An Amish Homecoming

MIRIAM BEILER

Contents

Chapter 1

E li gripped the reins of the borrowed horse-drawn buggy, white-knuckled. He rode down the familiar dusty lane towards the Zook family farm. The clip-clop of hooves and the gentle creak of wheels filled his ears, but they couldn't drown out the thundering of his heart. He'd been away for so long, chasing a life beyond the boundaries of his Amish community. Now, here he was, crawling back home with his tail between his legs.

As the buggy rounded the final bend, the sprawling farmhouse came into view. Eli's breath caught in his throat. It looked exactly the same – the white clapboard siding, the wrap-around porch, the red barn looming in the background. For a moment, he could almost believe the past seven years hadn't happened, that he was still the eager young man setting out on his rumspringa, ready to taste the English world.

But the illusion shattered as he caught sight of his father, Bishop Samuel Zook, standing ramrod straight on the porch. Even from a distance, Eli could feel the weight of his father's disapproving gaze. He swallowed hard, steadying himself for the confrontation to come.

Pulling the buggy to a stop, Eli climbed down, his legs feeling like lead. He approached the porch, hat in hand, trying to muster a smile. "Daed," he said softly, inclining his head in respect.

Samuel's face remained impassive, his steel-gray eyes boring into Eli. "So, you've decided to return," he said, his voice as cold and unyielding as a winter storm.

Eli nodded, fighting the urge to fidget under his father's scrutiny. "Jah, Daed. I... I've come home."

"Home," Samuel repeated, the word sounding like a rebuke. "We'll see about that. Your mother's inside. Go greet her."

Without another word, Samuel turned and strode into the barn, leaving Eli standing alone on the porch, feeling like a stranger in his own home. He took a deep breath, steeling himself before entering the house.

The familiar scent of fresh-baked bread and lemon polish enveloped him as he stepped inside. "Mamm?" he called out tentatively.

Sarah Zook appeared in the doorway to the kitchen, her eyes widening at the sight of her prodigal son. "Eli!" she exclaimed, rushing forward to embrace him. "Oh, my boy. You're home."

Eli melted into his mother's arms, feeling a lump form in his throat. "Jah, Mamm. I'm home."

The reunion with his mother was bittersweet, filled with tears and hesitant smiles. As night fell, Eli found himself in his old room, unpacking the few belongings he'd brought back with him. The space felt smaller than he remembered, the plain walls and simple furnishings so different from the life he'd led in the English world.

He ran his hand over the quilted bedspread, remembering countless nights spent dreaming of a life beyond

Lancaster County. Now, those dreams felt hollow, leaving him with nothing but regret and a desperate desire to make things right.

Unable to sleep, Eli slipped out of the house early the next morning. The farm was stirring to life, the sounds of roosters crowing and cows lowing filling the crisp autumn air. He walked through the fields, reacquainting himself with the land that had once been as familiar as his own heartbeat.

As he rounded a corner, he nearly collided with old Mr. Maas, his parents' neighbor. The elderly man's eyes widened in surprise. "Ach, if it isn't young Eli Zook! So the prodigal returns, eh?"

Eli felt his cheeks burn. "Gut morning, Mr. Maas. Jah, I've come home."

Mr. Maas's eyes twinkled with curiosity. "And will you be staying this time? Or is this just a visit?"

"I... I hope to stay," Eli replied, aware of the uncertainty in his voice. "If the community will have me."

The old man nodded sagely. "Well, you've got your work cut out for you, boy. But Gott is merciful, and so are His people. In time, perhaps."

As Mr. Maas ambled away, Eli couldn't shake the feeling that his return was already the subject of gossip throughout the community. He continued his walk, lost in thought, when a flash of blue caught his eye.

His heart skipped a beat as he recognized the figure walking along the creek. Hannah King - no, it would be Hannah Stoltzfus, now. He hadn't seen her in years, but even from a distance, he could see how she'd changed. Gone was the gangly girl he'd known; in her place was a poised woman, her grace evident even in the simple act of walking.

His mamm's letters over the years included births, deaths, and weddings as life in the community moved on without him. So Eli knew about her marriage, and then her husband's death. Jacob Stotlzfus had been a gut man.

Their eyes met across the field and she startled to a halt. Did she recognize him?

Eli was rooted to the spot, unsure whether to approach or flee. Hannah solved the dilemma for him, raising a hand in a tentative wave before continuing on her way.

Eli returned to the farm, his mind buzzing with conflicting emotions. The sight of Hannah stirred something in him—a longing for connection, for the life he'd left behind. But it also heightened his awareness of just how much of an outsider he'd become.

That evening, the community gathered for a hymn sing and potluck supper. Eli stood at the edge of the crowd, feeling every eye upon him. Whispers followed in his wake as he made his way to a seat, the weight of judgment heavy on his shoulders.

His father's voice rang out, leading the first hymn. Eli's throat tightened as he tried to join in, the once-familiar words feeling clumsy on his tongue. He glanced around, noting the easy camaraderie among the other young people—a circle he'd once been part of, now closed to him.

As the evening wore on, Eli found his gaze repeatedly drawn to Hannah. She moved through the gathering with quiet confidence, her smile warm and genuine as she greeted friends and neighbors. He noticed how her eyes crinkled at the corners when she laughed and the graceful way she tucked a stray strand of hair back under her kapp.

Lost in his observations, Eli didn't realize he'd drifted closer to a group of young men until he overheard their conversation.

"Did you see Eli Zook?" one of them muttered. "Can't believe he showed his face here after all this time."

"Jah, must think he can just waltz back in like nothing happened," another agreed.

"Well, he's in for a rude awakening if he thinks-"

The speaker cut off abruptly as he noticed Eli standing nearby. An awkward silence fell over the group, broken only when one of the young men cleared his throat and said, "Gut evening, Eli," before they all hurried away.

A hot flush of shame and anger crawled up Eli's neck as his cheeks burned. He'd known it wouldn't be easy, but the reality of his isolation hit him like a physical blow. He was seriously considering slipping away from the gathering when a soft voice behind him made him start.

"Wilkum home, Eli."

He turned to find Hannah standing there, a gentle smile on her face. "Hannah," he breathed, suddenly at a loss for words.

"It's gut to see you," she said, her eyes meeting his without judgment or suspicion. "How are you finding being back?"

Eli hesitated, torn between honesty and the desire to maintain his composure. "It's... an adjustment," he finally admitted.

Hannah nodded, understanding in her gaze. "I can only imagine. But I'm glad you're here. Many of us have been praying for your return."

Her words, spoken with such sincerity, touched something deep within Eli. For the first time since his arrival, he felt a glimmer of hope. "Danki, Hannah. That means more than you know."

They fell into an easy conversation, Hannah filling him in on some of the changes in the community since he'd left. As they talked, Eli felt some of the tension leave his body. Hannah's presence was like a balm, soothing the raw edges of his anxiety.

All too soon, Hannah was called away to help with serving the meal. As she left, she hovered a hand over Eli's arm, just shy of lightly touching his sleeve.

"Don't give up hope," she said softly. "Gott has a plan for all of us, even when we can't see it."

Eli watched her go, a strange warmth blooming in his chest. He'd come back to Lancaster County seeking redemption and a place to belong. He never expected to find a connection, let alone a reconnection with Hannah.

As the evening drew to a close, Eli found himself lingering, his eyes seeking out Hannah in the crowd. When their gazes met across the room, Hannah offered him a small smile that seemed to say, "You're not alone."

For the first time since his return, Eli felt a spark of something beyond anxiety and regret. It was small, fragile, but undeniably there.

A flicker of hope, of possibility. And as he climbed into the buggy for the ride home, that spark remained, a tiny light in the darkness of his uncertainty.

The road ahead would be long and difficult, Eli knew. Rebuilding trust, finding his place in the community once more—these were not tasks to be accomplished overnight. But as he glanced back at the gathering, catching one last glimpse of Hannah's retreating figure, he felt a renewed determination.

Maybe, just maybe, coming home hadn't been a mistake after all.

Chapter 2

Hannah's fingers brushed over the intricate stitching of the quilt spread before her, each careful movement practically second-nature after years of practice. The early morning sunlight streamed through the shop windows, casting a warm glow over the bolts of fabric lining the walls. As she worked, her mind wandered, the memories of Jacob that accompanied her every waking and sleeping hour were pushed aside. Instead, her mind pondered the utterly unexpected return of Eli Zook, home at last.

The bell above the door chimed, jolting Hannah from her reverie. She looked up to see Mary Lapp bustling in, her arms laden with a basket of freshly baked cinnamon rolls.

"Gut morning, Hannah!" Mary called out, her cheerful voice filling the quiet shop. "I thought we could use a treat today. It's been so busy lately."

Hannah smiled, gratitude washing over her. "Ach, Mary, you're too kind. They smell wunderbaar."

As Mary set the basket down and began arranging the rolls on a plate, Hannah's gaze drifted back to the quilt.

The pattern was one she'd started months ago, shortly after Jacob's passing. Its complexity had initially frustrated her, but now she found solace in the challenge.

"How are you holding up?" Mary asked softly, coming to stand beside Hannah. "I know this time of year must be especially difficult."

Hannah's hands stilled on the fabric. "It's... an adjustment," she admitted, echoing Eli's words from the day before. "Some days are easier than others."

Mary nodded sympathetically. "It's only been a year, Hannah. No one expects you to have it all figured out yet."

"I know," Hannah sighed. "But sometimes it feels like the whole community is holding its breath, waiting for me to... to move on."

As if on cue, the bell chimed again, and Mrs. Beiler, one of their regular customers, entered the shop. "Gut morning, girls!" she called out cheerfully. "My, it's a beautiful day, isn't it? Almost makes you want to fall in love all over again."

Hannah and Mary exchanged a glance, both recognizing the not-so-subtle hint in Mrs. Beiler's words. It wasn't the first time someone had made such a comment, and Hannah knew it wouldn't be the last.

"Jah, it is lovely out," Hannah replied politely, focusing on smoothing out a wrinkle in the quilt.

Mrs. Beiler browsed through the fabric selection, chattering away. "Did you hear? Eli Zook is back in town. I saw him at the general store this morning. My, how he's grown! Such a handsome young man now."

Hannah's heart skipped a beat at the mention of Eli's name. She bent her head, hoping the heat she felt rising in her cheeks wasn't visible.

"Is that so?" Mary replied, her tone carefully neutral. "Well, I'm sure his familye is glad to have him home."

"Oh, indeed," Mrs. Beiler continued, oblivious to Hannah's discomfort. "Though I hear things are a bit tense with his daed. But you know how it is! Never can be sure what's true and what's not."

Hannah suppressed a frown. Mrs. Beiler meant well, but she was quite prone to sharing gossip, despite how such a thing was discouraged. Instead of addressing it directly, though, Hannah just smiled politely and looked back down at her work.

As Mrs. Beiler continued to browse, Hannah found her mind drifting back to the previous evening. Eli's deep voice, his intense gaze, the way his presence made her feel both unsettled and oddly comforted. It had been so long since she'd felt that spark of... something.

Interest?

Attraction?

Surely not. The very thought made guilt twist in her stomach. Her Jacob, the love of her life, was hardly a year gone!

"Hannah?" Mary's gentle voice broke through her thoughts. "Are you alright? You look a million miles away."

Hannah blinked, realizing she'd been staring blankly at the quilt for several minutes. "Oh, jah. I'm fine. Just... thinking about this pattern. It's more challenging than I expected."

Mary's shrewd look told Hannah her friend wasn't entirely convinced, but she let it go. "Well, why don't we take a break? Those cinnamon rolls won't eat themselves."

Grateful for the distraction, Hannah followed Mary to the small table in the back of the shop. As they settled in with their treats and cups of steaming tea, Hannah found herself opening up.

"Mary," she began hesitantly, "do you ever feel... guilty for being happy? After-after bad things happen?"

Mary's eyes softened with understanding. "Oh, Hannah. Is that what's troubling you?"

Hannah nodded, her fingers tracing the rim of her teacup. "It's just... Jacob's been gone for a year now. And most days, I'm all right. My faith, my friends and familye ..."

She paused, dipping her head and smiling gratefully at Mary. "Those things brought me through the worst of it. I've found peace in my work, in our community. But lately..."

"Lately?" Mary prompted gently when Hannah trailed off.

"Lately, I've been feeling... restless," Hannah admitted. "Like maybe I'm ready for something more. But then I think of Jacob, and I feel so... disloyal. Like I'm betraying him. Betraying us."

Mary reached across the table, squeezing Hannah's hand. "Hannah, listen to me. Jacob loved you more than anything in this world. Do you really think he'd want you to spend the rest of your life alone and unhappy?"

Hannah shook her head, feeling tears prick at her eyes. "Nee, I know he wouldn't. But it's not just that. It's... well, it's Eli."

Mary's eyebrows shot up. "Eli Zook? What about him?"

Hannah took a deep breath, the words tumbling out in a rush. "I saw him yesterday, at the hymn sing. We talked, only for a few moments. But it was... nice."

Her cheeks flushed pink. "More than nice. And now I can't stop thinking about him, and I feel terrible because it's only been a year since Jacob's accident, and Eli's only just come back! He's not even fully committed or baptized and-"

"Ach, slow down," Mary interrupted, a smile playing at her lips. "Hannah, it's okay to have feelings. It doesn't make you disloyal to Jacob's memory. It makes you human."

Hannah sighed, slumping back in her chair. "I know you're right. But it's all so confusing. I barely know Eli anymore. And even if I did want to... explore these feelings, I don't know if he'd be interested. Or if the community would approve."

"Well, from what I saw last night, Eli seemed plenty interested," Mary said with a wink. "And as for the community, they've been pushing you to move on for months now. Though I doubt they expected it to be with the bishop's own prodigal son himself. He's like the story straight from the Bible!"

Hannah couldn't help but laugh at that, some of the tension easing from her shoulders. "Oh, Mary. You do know there was more than one son in that story, jah?"

She sighed, lighter now she'd gotten everything off her chest. Hannah smiled at her friend, reaching out to squeeze Mary's hand. "Whatever would I do without you?"

"Probably wallow in guilt and confusion," Mary teased. "Now, eat your cinnamon roll before it gets cold and hard. We've got a busy day ahead of us."

As they finished their impromptu breakfast and returned to work, Hannah felt lighter. The guilt and confusion weren't gone entirely, but talking with Mary had helped put things in perspective.

The morning passed in a flurry of activity. Several young women came in to choose fabrics for their wedding quilts, and Hannah found herself offering advice and sharing in their excitement. It was bittersweet, remembering her own wedding preparations, but she was surprised to find the memories brought more warmth than pain, today.

As lunchtime approached, the shop quieted down. Hannah was just considering closing up for a quick break when the bell chimed once more. She looked up, her heart leaping into her throat as she saw Eli Zook himself standing in the doorway.

"Gut day," Eli said, his deep voice sending a shiver down Hannah's spine. "I hope I'm not interrupting at a bad time."

"Nee, not at all," Hannah managed, acutely aware of Mary's curious gaze. "How can we help you?"

Eli stepped further into the shop, his eyes never leaving Hannah's. "I'm actually here to pick up an order for my mamm. She mentioned something about new fabric."

"Oh, of course," Hannah said, grateful for something to do with her hands. She bustled behind the counter, retrieving the package of fabric she'd set aside earlier that week. "Here you are. I hope it's to her liking."

As she handed over the package, their fingers brushed, and Hannah felt a jolt of electricity at the contact. Eli's eyes widened slightly, and she knew he'd felt it too.

"Danki," Eli said softly. He hesitated for a moment, then added, "I was wondering... would you like to take a walk sometime? To catch up properly?"

Hannah's breath caught in her throat. This was it—the moment she'd both dreaded and longed for. A chance to explore these new, confusing feelings. A step towards something... more.

But as she opened her mouth to respond, a wave of guilt washed over her. Images of Jacob flashed through her mind. His kind smile, his gentle touch, the life they'd planned together. How could she even consider moving on?

"I... I don't know if that's a good idea," Hannah said, her voice barely above a whisper. "I'm sorry, Eli. It's just, I mean. I just..." She looked away, shoulders curling up towards her ears.

"I don't think that's a good idea. Maybe another time?" she finished with a feeble smile.

Disappointment flickered in Eli's eyes, but he nodded with a look of understanding. "Of course. I shouldn't have presumed. Take all the time you need, Hannah. I'll be here when you're ready... if you're ever ready."

With a final nod, Eli turned and left the shop. Hannah watched him go, her heart pounding. She'd done the right thing, hadn't she? Honoring Jacob's memory, not rushing into anything?

But as she turned back to her work, Hannah couldn't shake the feeling that she'd just let something precious slip through her fingers. The quilt before her suddenly mocked her with its intricate pattern. The challenge was no longer inviting, but instead daunting.

As the afternoon wore on, Hannah found herself stealing glances at the door, half-hoping Eli would return. But he didn't, of course. With each passing hour, the weight of her decision settled more heavily on her shoulders. Finally, Hannah locked up for the evening and trudged home.

That evening, as Hannah prepared for bed, she found herself standing before the carved box Jacob gifted her when they were courting. She kept it on her dresser, with a few mementos like dried flowers he'd picked for her saved inside, in a mirror of the box's outsides.

"Oh, Jacob," she whispered, tracing the flowers he'd lovingly carved with her fingertips. "What am I supposed to do? How do I honor your memory while still living my life?"

Of course, no one answered. But as Hannah climbed into bed, she prayed.

Something was shifting, and she didn't know what to do about it. Gott would show her the way, He always did. But how long would that take?

The spark of connection she'd felt with Eli, the way her heart had raced at his nearness—it was a feeling she hadn't experienced since before Jacob's death.

As she drifted off to sleep, Hannah's last thoughts thrilled and terrified her: she was falling for Eli Zook. And she had no idea what to do about it.

Could she find a new path, a new love with *him*?

With Eli, who left?

With Eli, who came home.

But... how long would he stay?

Chapter 3

Eli's muscles burned as he swung the scythe, the blade slicing through the golden wheat with a satisfying swish. The morning sun beat down on his back, sweat soaking through his shirt as he worked alongside the other men in the field. He could feel their eyes on him, watching, evaluating.

Every cut of the scythe was a statement: I belong here. I can do this. I am back.

To his left, Samuel Zook worked with the efficiency of years of practice, his movements fluid and purposeful. Eli stole a glance at his father, searching for any sign of approval, but Samuel's face remained impassive, focused solely on the task at hand.

"Gut job, Eli," John Lapp called out, pausing to wipe his brow. "You haven't lost your touch after all these years in the English world."

Eli nodded his thanks, warmth spreading through his chest at the small acknowledgment. "The work may be different out there," he replied, "but hard work is hard work, no matter where you are."

A murmur of agreement rippled through the group of men. Eli felt a flicker of hope. Maybe he really could find his place here again.

The sound of approaching horses and clattering wheels drew their attention. Eli's heart skipped a beat as he saw the group of women arriving with baskets of food and jugs of water. His eyes scanned the crowd, searching for one face in particular.

There she was. Hannah Stoltzfus, her kapp neatly in place, a basket balanced on her hip. As if sensing his gaze, she looked up, their eyes meeting across the field. Eli felt a jolt of electricity run through him, nearly dropping his scythe.

"Careful there, son," Samuel's gruff voice broke through Eli's reverie. "Keep your mind on your work."

Eli nodded, face flushing as he returned to his task. But he couldn't help stealing glances as Hannah and the other women set up tables at the edge of the field, laying out a spread of sandwiches, pies, and cool drinks.

As the morning wore on, Eli threw himself into the work with renewed vigor. He was determined to prove himself, not just to his father and the community, but to Hannah as well.

The rhythm of the harvest took over—cut, gather, bind. Cut, gather, bind. The stack of wheat sheaves grew steadily behind him.

"Alright, men," Samuel called out as the sun reached its zenith. "Time for a break. Let's see what the women have prepared for us."

Eli's heart raced as they approached the tables. Hannah was there, ladling out cups of cool lemonade. Their eyes met again as she handed him a cup, her fingers brushing against his.

"Danki," Eli murmured, his voice suddenly hoarse.

"You're welcome," Hannah replied softly. "You've been working hard out there."

Eli nodded, searching for something more to say. "It feels gut to be back in the fields. I... I've missed this."

Hannah's eyes softened. "I'm glad. The community has missed you, Eli."

Before Eli could respond, and thankfully before he said something brash, like asking if *she* missed him, his father appeared at his side.

"Hannah," he said, his tone cordial but cool. "Thank you for helping with the meal. Your mother would be proud of how well you've stepped into her role."

Hannah ducked her head modestly. "Danki, Bishop Zook. I'm just doing what needs to be done."

As Samuel moved on, Eli found himself alone with Hannah once more. He took a sip of lemonade, gathering his courage. "Hannah, I was wondering if-"

"Eli!" John Lapp called out. "Come join us! We want to hear about your time in the English world."

Eli hesitated, torn between his desire to talk with Hannah and the need to connect with the other men.

Hannah gave him a small smile. "Go on," she said. "We can talk later. Promise."

With a nod, Eli joined the group of men, answering their questions about his experiences outside the community. As he spoke, he sensed Hannah watching him from across the gathering. He glanced back and smiled at her, waving. She waved back as a thoughtful expression crossed her lovely face.

Hannah busied herself with refilling empty plates and cups, but her attention kept drifting to Eli. She marveled at the changes in him, drawn to the man he'd become.

The gangly boy she remembered had grown into a strong, confident man. His deep voice carried across the gathering as he shared stories of his time away, his hands moving animatedly as he spoke.

"He's certainly changed, hasn't he?" Mary Lapp murmured, appearing at Hannah's side.

Hannah startled, nearly dropping the pitcher of lemonade. "I... I suppose he has," she managed, feeling her cheeks warm.

Mary's knowing smile made Hannah's blush deepen. "It's all right to notice, you know," her friend said gently. "It's been over a year since Jacob passed. No one would blame you for having feelings."

Hannah shook her head, pushing down the guilt that rose at the mention of her late husband. "It's not like that," she protested weakly. "I'm just... curious about how he's changed, that's all."

"Mmhmm," Mary hummed, unconvinced. "Well, whatever it is, just be careful. Not everyone is as happy about Eli's return as you seem to be."

Following Mary's gaze, Hannah noticed Bishop Zook watching his son with a guarded expression. The older man's disapproval was clear, even from a distance.

As the break came to an end and the men prepared to return to the fields, Hannah found herself gravitating towards Eli once more. He was gathering empty plates, his strong hands making quick work of the task.

"Here, let me help," Hannah offered, reaching for a stack of dishes.

Their hands brushed again, and Hannah's breath caught. That same spark of electricity...

Eli's eyes met hers, and for a moment, the world faded away.

"Danki," Eli said softly. "For everything. The food, the help... and for being so welcoming."

Hannah's heart fluttered at the sincerity in his voice. "Of course," she replied. "It's gut to have you back, Eli. Truly."

A shadow fell across them, and Hannah looked up to see Bishop Zook approaching. "Time to get back to work, Eli," he said, his tone leaving no room for argument.

Eli nodded, his expression sobering. "Yes, Daed. I'll be right there."

As Eli turned to go, Hannah found herself calling out, "Eli!" He paused, looking back at her expectantly. "I... I hope we can talk more later. Maybe after the harvest is done?"

A slow smile spread across Eli's face, warming Hannah from the inside out. "I'd like that," he said. "Very much."

As Eli jogged back to the fields, Hannah couldn't ignore the way her heart raced. She watched him go, a maelstrom of emotions swirling within her. Attraction and guilt, hope and fear.

They all tangled together inside her chest.

"Be careful, child," a gentle voice said. Hannah turned to see Sarah Zook, Eli's mother, standing nearby. "The heart is a fragile thing, especially when it's still healing."

Hannah nodded, unable to deny the truth in Sarah's words. "I know," she said softly. "I'm not... I don't even know what I'm feeling. It's all so confusing."

Sarah's eyes were kind as she patted Hannah's arm. "I meant Eli's heart, as much as your own. But, just give it time," she advised. "Gott has a plan for all of us, even when we can't see it clearly."

As the afternoon wore on, Eli's form continually drew Hannah's gaze. She watched as he worked tirelessly in the fields, impressing even the most skeptical of the men with his strength and skill. There was something different about him now – a quiet confidence that wasn't there before he left.

When the sun began to dip towards the horizon, signaling the end of the day's work, Hannah's throat went dry. She'd been looking forward to talking with Eli again, but now that the moment was approaching, nervousness fluttered in her stomach.

As the men made their way back from the fields, Hannah busied herself with packing up the remaining food and cleaning the tables. She could hear Eli's voice among the others, laughing at something John Lapp had said.

"Hannah?"

She looked up to find Eli standing before her, his hair tousled from the day's work, a sheen of sweat still glistening on his brow. Hannah's breath caught in her throat.

"Eli," she managed. "You... you did well out there today."

He smiled, the corners of his eyes crinkling in a way that made Hannah's heart skip. "Danki. It felt gut to be back in the fields. Almost like I never left."

An awkward silence fell between them, heavy with unspoken words and emotions. Hannah fidgeted with the edge of her apron, searching for something to say.

"I was wondering," Eli began, his voice low and hesitant, "if you'd like to take that walk sometime? Maybe tomorrow evening, after the day's work is done?"

Hannah's heart raced. She should say no...

It was still too soon. Wasn't it? But she didn't want to reject the offer, not again.

Hannah suspected that people would talk. But looking into Eli's earnest face, she found herself nodding. "I'd like that," she said softly.

Eli's face lit up with a smile that made Hannah's knees weak. "Gut," he said. "I'll meet you by the big oak tree at the edge of our property, just after supper?"

"I'll be there," Hannah promised.

As Eli turned to go, helping the other men load the last of the equipment onto the wagon, Hannah caught sight of Bishop Zook watching them from across the field. His expression was unreadable, but there was a tension in his posture that made Hannah uneasy.

She bit her lower lip. Whatever was growing between her and Eli, it wouldn't be simple.

There were wounds that needed healing, not just in her heart, but in Eli's family and the community as well. And yet, as she watched Eli climb onto the wagon, throwing one last smile her way, Hannah's heart lit up with a spark of hope.

Perhaps, she thought, this was Gott's plan all along. A chance for healing, for new beginnings. As Hannah gathered her things and prepared to head home, she sent up a silent prayer, asking for guidance and strength for whatever lay ahead.

The sun dipped below the horizon, painting the sky in brilliant shades of orange and pink. Hannah took a deep breath, inhaling the scent of freshly harvested wheat and the promise of autumn in the air. Tomorrow would bring a new day, and with it, a chance to explore these newfound feelings. For the first time in a long while, Hannah found herself looking forward to what the future might hold.

Chapter 4

Eli's palms were sweating as he pushed open the door to Hannah's quilt shop, the little bell above tinkling merrily. The scent of freshly pressed fabric and lavender sachet enveloped him, reminding him of his mamm's sewing room. His eyes scanned the colorful bolts of fabric lining the walls, feeling overwhelmed by the choices.

The evening before, they'd walked along the fields, side-by-side. He hardly recalled what they talked about, only that conversation flowed easily. It was so natural, talking with Hannah.

She was open to his overtures, but he still hadn't joined the community officially. Was he being unfair to her? Should he have waited longer before asking her to spend time with him? Theirs was a more open community than some Amish, but still...

He wasn't courting her officially, couldn't as he wasn't part of the congregation officially. Not yet. But Eli wanted nothing more than to be baptized and fully join the church for good. Then, he could ask to court Hannah, properly.

His father, though... Samuel Zook required more than simple professions. Eli was well into his instruction classes, but he'd have to convince his father before Eli could make his confession of faith and truly join.

"Gut afternoon, Eli," Hannah's soft voice called out from behind the counter. "It's nice to see you again. Can I help you with something?"

Eli's heart skipped a beat as he turned to face her. Hannah's warm hazel eyes met his, a gentle smile playing on her lips. He swallowed hard, suddenly forgetting why he'd come.

"I, uh... Mamm needs some fabric for mending," he managed, running a hand through his hair. In truth, he suspected she'd manufactured the errand, giving the twinkle in his mamm's eye when she declared a 'sewing emergency.' Not that he was complaining.

"But I'm not sure what to choose."

Hannah's smile widened as she came around the counter. "Well, let's see what we can find. What color did she have in mind?"

As Hannah led him through the shop, Eli watched the grace with which she moved, the way her kapp framed her face just so. He shook his head, trying to focus on the task at hand.

"She mentioned something blue, I think," Eli said, his eyes drawn to a bolt of sky-blue fabric. "Maybe something like this?"

Hannah nodded approvingly. "That's a lovely choice. It would make beautiful curtains or a nice dress."

As she reached for the fabric, her hand brushed against Eli's. A jolt of warmth shot through him at the contact, and he saw Hannah's cheeks flush pink. For a moment, neither of them moved, their hands lingering together on the bolt of fabric, just touching.

Hannah broke the silence with a soft laugh, pulling her hand away. "Do you remember when we were kinner, and we'd play hide and seek in the cornfields?"

Eli grinned, grateful for the distraction. "Jah, I do. You were always the best at finding the perfect hiding spots."

"And you were always the one who'd get so excited when you found someone, you'd yelp and give away your position to everyone else," Hannah teased.

They both laughed, the tension easing between them. As Hannah began to measure and cut the fabric, Eli found himself relaxing, sharing more childhood memories.

"Remember that time we tried to catch fireflies in jars?" he asked, leaning against the counter.

Hannah's eyes sparkled with mirth. "Oh jah, and you tripped over a root and fell face-first into the creek!"

"Hey now," Eli protested, chuckling. "I was trying to catch a particularly elusive firefly. It wasn't my fault the ground was uneven."

As they continued to reminisce, neither noticed Mary Lapp watching them from the back of the shop, a knowing smile on her face.

Hannah's heart was racing as she finished wrapping Eli's purchase. Their easy laughter and shared memories, on the heels of the lovely walk the previous evening, awakened feelings she thought long buried. As she handed him the package, their fingers brushed yet again, sending a shiver down her spine.

"Danki, Hannah," Eli said softly, his deep brown eyes holding hers. "I'm glad I came in today."

"Me too," Hannah replied, her voice barely above a whisper. She cleared her throat and, hardly believing her own daring, asked, "Will I see you at the singing tonight?"

Eli nodded, a smile spreading across his face. "Jah, I'll be there. Save me a seat?"

As the door closed behind him, Hannah let out her breath with a whoosh. How long had she even been holding it? She turned to find Mary watching her, eyebrows raised.

"Don't say it," Hannah warned, feeling her cheeks grow warm.

Mary held up her hands in mock surrender. "I didn't say a word. But if I were going to say something, well. I might mention how your face lights up when he's around. You look happy, Hannah." Her friend smiled at her, soft and kind.

Hannah busied herself straightening bolts of fabric, trying to ignore the flutter in her stomach. "It's not like that. We're just... reconnecting as friends," she said, the words weak even to her ears.

"Mmhmm," Mary hummed, unconvinced. "Well, whatever it is you're doing with Eli, it's nice to see you smiling again. I'm glad he came back."

So am I.

As the afternoon wore on, Hannah found her thoughts continually drifting to Eli. She was excited, but a little guilty at how excited, about the prospect of seeing him at the singing. Part of her longed to explore these new feelings, while another part started castigating her.

I'm not betraying Jacob. Not our marriage, not his memory, she told herself, pushing back against the rising tide of guilt snapping on the heels of that wave of excitement.

When evening fell, Hannah closed up the shop and made her way to the community gathering place where the singing was set to be. The large room was already filled with familiar faces, the buzz of conversation filling the air. Her eyes scanned the crowd, searching for Eli.

"Looking for someone?" a deep voice asked from behind her.

Hannah turned to find Eli standing there, a warm smile on his face. Her heart skipped a beat as she took in his neatly pressed shirt and freshly shaven face.

"I saved you a seat," she managed, gesturing to an empty space on the bench beside her.

As they sat down, Hannah was acutely aware of Eli's presence. The warmth of his arm was close enough for her to feel. If she leaned only a little bit to the right, she'd press right up against him. The scent of soap and fresh air, and something else... something wholly masculine, clung to him. She tried to focus on the hymns, but found herself stealing glances at Eli throughout the evening.

Once, their eyes met during a particularly moving verse, and Hannah drowned in his eyes, lost and found at the same time as the rest of the room faded away. There was something in Eli's gaze that called to her heart—an answering depth of emotion that both thrilled and terrified her.

Chapter 5

A t the singing, Eli's deep voice faltered at first as he struggled to recall half-forgotten words. But as the evening progressed, his voice grew stronger and more assured.

He was buoyed by Hannah's presence beside him. Somehow, he'd forgotten how much he enjoyed these community gatherings, the way all the voices blended in harmony, praising Gott together.

As the final note faded away, peace settled over Eli, Gott's love embracing him. He swallowed, throat tight with emotion as the bone-deep certainty he was finally on the right path filled his soul. He turned to Hannah, finding her eyes already on him.

"That was wunderbaar," he said softly.

Hannah nodded, a gentle smile playing on her lips. "It's always been one of my favorite hymns."

As the group began to disperse, someone suggested a walk under the stars. Eli's heart thumped at the opportunity to spend more time with Hannah. They joined the small group heading outside, the cool October air nipping at their cheeks.

Eli and Hannah fell into step together, slightly behind the others. Their hands swung close as they walked, pinkies once brushing against each other. The accidental touch sent a jolt through Eli's body.

He forced himself to take half a step to the left. If he hadn't, the next touch of their hands wouldn't be accidental.

"So," Eli began, searching for a safe topic. "How's business at the quilt shop?"

Hannah's face lit up as she spoke about her work, describing the new patterns she was developing and the satisfaction of advising and teaching younger girls about quilting. Eli was captivated by her passion. Her hands flew through the air, graceful as swooping birds and the way her eyes sparkled as she talked... he stared, half-smiling at how charming she was, without any effort at all.

His heart thumped. Eli was in over his head. Well, head over heels in love with her.

"I'm sorry," Hannah said suddenly, ducking her head. "I'm rambling on about quilts. You must be bored."

Eli shook his head emphatically. "Nee, not at all. I love hearing you talk about something you care about so much."

Their eyes met, and Eli forgot everything. Forgot they were outside, under the stars and skies where Gott and anyone glancing back from the group would see them.

Everything narrowed to the beautiful woman in front of him. His hand twitched. Without thinking, he reached out, brushing a stray wisp of hair back under Hannah's kapp. Eli's fingertips lingered, cupping her cheek gently with the calloused pads of his first two fingers.

Hannah's breath hitched, her eyes wide as they locked onto Eli's. Everything else disappeared—the group ahead of them, the chirping crickets, even the stars above. There was only Hannah, her soft skin under his palm, her lips slightly parted as she stared up at him, eyes wide and luminous as the moon.

"Eli! Hannah!" a voice called out, shattering the moment. "Aren't you two coming?"

They jumped apart, both flushing deep red. Eli's heart was pounding as they hurried to catch up with the group, acutely aware of what had almost happened. Thank the Lord the others were around the bend in the path ahead and hadn't seen...

What was wrong with him? She deserved better.

Hannah's mind was reeling as they rejoined the others. The feeling of Eli's hand on her cheek lingered, sending shivers down her spine. Hannah swore the heat from his touch lingered on her skin, and she pressed her own fingertips to the spot on her cheek he'd touched.

She snuck a sidelong glance at Eli, mouth going dry as she found his dark eyes already on her. The intensity of his gaze made her breath catch.

As they walked back to the gathering place, Hannah's emotions warred within her. The excitement of this new connection with Eli clashed with a resurgence of guilt over moving on from Jacob like this. She shouldn't have done that. Should have stepped back as soon as he'd lifted a hand to her face.

Instead... she'd enjoyed his touch on her cheek, had been half a second from leaning into it, from lifting her own hand and pressing his palm to fully cup her face. It was all wrong.

They weren't married. They weren't courting.

Eli wasn't even a full member of the church yet. She twisted her hands together, torn between what her heart wanted and what she felt was right.

"Are you cold?" Eli asked softly, noticing her agitation.

Hannah shook her head, forcing a smile. "Nee, I'm fine. Just... thinking."

Eli's brow furrowed with concern. "About what?"

She hesitated, unsure how to express the turmoil inside her. "It's just... this is all happening so fast. I'm not sure if I'm ready for..." she trailed off, unable to find the right words.

Understanding dawned in Eli's eyes. He nodded slowly, his expression stormy with disappointment he couldn't hide.

The barest smile flickered over his face, then vanished, though she could hear the compassion in his voice. "I understand, Hannah. We-we should take things slow. I don't want to pressure you into anything you're not comfortable with. I shouldn't have pressed like that. I'm sorry."

Relief washed over Hannah, along with a twinge of regret. Part of her wanted to throw caution to the wind, to explore these feelings with Eli. But the larger part knew she needed time to sort through her emotions and time to pray for guidance.

"Danki, Eli," she said softly. "For understanding."

As they reached the gathering place, Hannah felt the weight of curious eyes upon them. She realized with a start that their slower pace and brief absence hadn't gone unnoticed.

The blood drained from her face. Hannah blinked rapidly, gaze darting from face to face. Had anyone seen...?

When she finally reached her friend, Mary caught her eye, raising an eyebrow in silent question.

"Well, this was a lovely evening," Hannah said, perhaps a bit too brightly. "But I should be getting home. I have an early start at the shop tomorrow."

Eli nodded, a hint of sadness in his eyes. "Of course. May I walk you home?"

Hannah hesitated, torn between wanting more time with Eli and needing space to think. "That's very kind of you, but I'll be fine. It's not far."

"Ah, of course," Eli conceded. "Gut night, Hannah. Sleep well."

As Hannah walked home alone, her mind raced with conflicting thoughts. The memory of Eli's touch, the warmth in his eyes, the way he made her laugh.

It all filled her with a joy, a lightness and warmth she hadn't felt in so long. Like the returning sunshine of spring after a long winter of pale, cold sunlight.

But alongside that joy was a gnawing guilt. Was it too soon? What would Jacob think what happened just a little while ago?

She paused at her front door, looking up at the star-filled sky. "Oh, Jacob," she whispered. "What am I supposed to do?"

Eli watched Hannah's retreating figure as she disappeared into the darkness. His heart was heavy, the exhilaration and giddiness replaced by leaden disappointment.

He understood Hannah's hesitation—her loss was not so long ago fresh, and he knew the community would have opinions about their budding relationship. But he couldn't deny the connection he felt with her, stronger than anything he'd experienced before.

"Everything all right, son?" Bishop Zook's voice startled Eli from his thoughts.

Eli turned to find his father watching him with a close look. He felt his cheeks warm, wondering how much his daed had seen.

"Jah, Daed," Eli replied, trying to keep his voice steady. "Just... enjoying the evening."

Samuel Zook's eyes narrowed slightly. "I see. And does this enjoyment have anything to do with Hannah Stoltzfus?"

Eli's heart raced. He'd known this conversation was coming, but he was still, somehow, completely unprepared. "Hannah and I are friends, Daed. We've been reconnecting since I came home."

"Hmm," Samuel hummed, his expression unreadable. "Be careful, Eli. Hannah's still grieving, and you... well, you've only just returned to us. The community will be watching closely. You should wait until after your baptism to start anything. Assuming, of course, you still want that."

Eli bristled at the doubt in his father's voice. But, could he blame him? The bishop's only son, and he'd run off on rumspringa the first chance he got... and never returned. Not until he tired of the hollow Englisher world. Not until he learned what his father always warned him against, that the world outside wouldn't fulfill Eli.

Eli nodded, frustration and understanding washing over him. "I do, and I know, Daed. We're taking things slow. We're friends," he reiterated, as if trying to convince himself.

But... that wasn't quite true, was it? Eli didn't think of her as just a friend. Anyone with eyes could see that.

And he certainly wasn't treating her like a friend. As he and his father traveled home together, Eli's mind whirled with possibilities.

He knew the path ahead wouldn't be easy, but something in his heart told him Hannah was worth it. He just needed to prove to her—and to the community—that he was here to stay, that his feelings were genuine. Eli didn't want to step back, didn't want to pull away from the warmth and light that was Hannah Stoltzfus.

Climbing into bed that night, Eli found himself unable to sleep. Every time he closed his eyes, he saw Hannah's face, felt the softness of her cheek under his fingertips. He tossed and turned, his heart and mind at war.

Giving up on sleep, he gave himself over to Gott, praying and pleading for wisdom. What should he do?

Finally, hours later, only a little while before the first light of dawn would soon creep through his window, Eli came to a decision. He would give Hannah the time and space she needed, but he wouldn't give up. He'd show her, day by day, that his intentions were honorable, that his feelings were true.

With that resolve, Eli finally drifted off to sleep, dreaming of hazel eyes, a warm hand in his, and chiming laughter under a starry, moonlit sky.

Chapter 6

Eli's muscles strained as he hefted another bale of hay onto the wagon. The crisp November air bit at his cheeks, but sweat still beaded on his brow from the exertion. He paused, wiping his forehead with his sleeve, and surveyed the field. They were making good progress, but there was still much to be done before winter set in.

"Eli!" John Lapp called from across the field. "Where do you want these pumpkins?"

Eli jogged over, his mind already calculating the best use of space. "Let's stack them by the barn," he decided. "We can sort through them later, see which ones are still gut for market."

John nodded approvingly. "Smart thinking. You've really taken charge here."

A small spark of pride flickered in Eli's chest, quickly tamped down by humility. "Just doing what needs to be done," he replied modestly.

As they worked, Eli caught from the corner of his eye a few approving glances from some of the other men. It felt gut to be useful, to be part of the community again.

But even as he directed the work, his mind kept drifting to Hannah. The memory of her soft laugh, the way her eyes crinkled when she smiled. His heart raced.

"Eli!" His father's stern voice cut through his daydreams. "A word, please."

Eli's stomach clenched as he made his way to where the bishop stood, arms crossed and brow furrowed. "Jah, Daed?"

"What's this I hear about you wanting to try new farming methods?" Samuel demanded. "We've been doing things the same way for generations. It's worked just fine."

Eli took a deep breath, steeling himself. "I've been reading about crop rotation and soil conservation, Daed. I think it could really improve our yields."

Samuel's frown deepened. "Reading where? Where did you get these ideas?"

"From books at the library in town," Eli admitted. "I know it's not our usual way, but-"

"Not our *usual* way? More like never our way," Samuel interrupted. "We don't need English ideas when our methods work perfectly well. We stick to what we know, Eli. What we've always done."

As his father walked away, Eli clenched a fist and his jaw. He breathed in, then out slowly as frustration bubbled up inside him. He was right about this.

But how could he convince his father to listen?

Hannah hummed as she selected the next piece of fabric, stitching together pieces of Jacob's old shirts into a beautiful pattern. The memory quilt was coming together nicely, each square a lovely reminder of her late husband.

But as she worked, guilt gnawed at her heart. Why was she thinking about Eli while she worked on this tangible reminder of Jacob? She swallowed around the thickness half-closing off her throat as her eyes welled.

A knock at the door startled her from her thoughts. "Come in," she called, hastily wiping away a stray tear.

Mary poked her head in, a concerned look on her face. "Hannah? Are you alright?"

Hannah forced a smile. "Jah, I'm fine. Just working on Jacob's quilt."

Mary settled into a chair beside her, eyeing the quilt with admiration. "It's beautiful, Hannah. Jacob would have loved it."

"Do you really think so?" Hannah asked, her voice barely above a whisper.

"Of course," Mary assured her. She fixed her friend with a compassionate look and sat beside her. "You look so sad still, my freind. Conflicted. Hannah... you know he would want you to be happy, right? To move on?"

Hannah's hands stilled on the quilt. "I know," she said softly. "It's just... complicated."

Mary's eyes softened with understanding. "Because of Eli?"

Hannah's cheeks flushed and she ducked her head a little, not meeting Mary's too-knowing eyes. "Ach, how did you know?" she muttered.

"Come, come now," Mary teased gently. "Anyone with eyes can see the way you two look at each other. It's sweet."

"It's not gut, not-not *right*,," Hannah protested weakly. "It's still too soon and he's not even committed to our way of life. What would people think?"

Mary's expression turned serious. "Hannah, listen to me. You can't live your life worrying about what others think. Gott knows your heart. If He's put these feelings for Eli there in your heart, who are we to question it?"

Hannah sighed, her fingers tracing the outline of a shirt piece that had been Jacob's favorite. "I just... I feel so guilty. I should honor Jacob's memory. Like with this quilt. But even now... I keep thinking about Eli!" she said, distressed.

"Moving on doesn't mean forgetting," Mary said gently. "Jacob will always be a part of you. But he wouldn't want you to be alone forever. Now," she said, standing and patting Hannah's shoulder. "I have to finish a few errands, but you think about what I said. Don't fret, and let yourself be happy, Hannah."

As Mary left, Hannah's mind whirled with conflicting emotions. She remembered the warmth of Eli's smile, the way his presence made her feel safe and cherished.

But then she looked down at the quilt in her lap, each scrap of fabric, every last stitch another memento of the life she'd shared with Jacob. A life she had expected, had *wanted* to last forever... a life that came crashing down far too soon.

"Gott, please," she whispered, closing her eyes as a few tears trickled down her cheeks. "How do I know what's right or wrong anymore? Please. Share Your wisdom and guidance with me."

After a few moments, she opened her eyes and sighed. Gott would answer in His own time. She'd trust in Him.

But for now, the quilt deserved her time and attention. With a heavy heart, Hannah returned to her sewing.

But try as she might, she couldn't shake Eli's handsome smile from her mind.

After he got home, Eli found his mother in the kitchen, kneading dough for the evening's bread. The familiar scent of yeast and flour filled the air, bringing back memories of his childhood. He hesitated in the doorway, suddenly a small boy again, seeking comfort from his mamm after a hard day.

"Mamm?" he said softly. "Can I talk to you about something?"

Sarah looked up, her hands covered in flour. "Of course, Eli. What's troubling you?"

Eli settled onto a kitchen chair, running a hand through his hair. "It's... it's Hannah," he admitted. "I can't stop thinking about her."

Sarah's eyes softened with understanding. "Ach, I see. And how does she feel about you?"

"I'm not sure," Eli sighed. "Sometimes I think she might feel the same way, but then she pulls away. I know it's complicated with Jacob and my situation in the community and all, but..."

"But your heart wants what it wants," Sarah finished for him. She wiped her hands on her apron and sat down across from him. "Eli, love is never simple. But Gott brought you back home. Gott put these feelings in your heart. You shouldn't just ignore them."

Eli looked at his mother, hope blooming in his chest. "You really think so? You don't think it's too soon?"

Sarah reached out, patting his hand. "Only Hannah can decide that. But I've seen the way you look at her. And the way she looks at you when she thinks no one's watching. Give it time, sohn. Be patient and kind. If it's meant to be, it will happen."

Eli nodded, feeling a weight lift from his shoulders. "Danki, Mamm. I don't know what I'd do without you."

Sarah smiled, her eyes twinkling. "Well, for starters, you'd probably starve. Now, make yourself useful and help me with these loaves."

As they worked side by side, Eli breathed in a renewed sense of hope. Maybe, just maybe, there was a chance for him and Hannah after all.

Obstacles stood in their way, as with all things in life. Though...the obstacle that was Bishope Samuel Zook was a difficult man, fierce in the protection and care of the community entrusted to him by Gott. He wouldn't allow even his own son to join without being fully convinced of his commitment to both the faith and the community as a whole, let alone give his blessing for Eli and Hannah before all of that was sorted out.

But Eli wasn't worried. He was back for good.

And soon enough, he'd convince his daed of that truth as well.

Chapter 7

Hannah's heart picked up speed as she approached the Zook farm, a basket of freshly baked oatmeal cookies in her arms. She'd spent the morning baking, telling herself it was just a neighborly gesture. But deep down, she knew she was hoping to catch a glimpse of Eli.

As she neared the house, she heard voices coming from the barn. Oh yes, that must be the women's circle Sarah Zook ran.

She'd not attended since losing Jacob, and only half-heartedly before then, being quite busy at her shop. But curiosity got the better of her, and she drifted closer, detouring form her destination for a few moments.

"...spending an awful lot of time looking at that Hannah Stoltzfus," a woman's voice drifted out. "Don't you think it's a bit soon?"

"Well, we've all been encouraging her to move on," another voice replied. "But with Eli Zook? After everything that happened when he left? Now, that's not the kind of choice I'd expect from an upstanding woman like her.

How do we even know he'll stay? She'll end up breaking her own heart at this rate."

Hannah froze, her cheeks burning with embarrassment and anger. Were people really gossiping about her and Eli?

At the bishop's own home? What happened to gossip being looked down upon?

Before she could retreat, Eli himself rounded the corner of the barn. His face lit up when he saw her, and Hannah felt her heart skip a beat.

"Hannah," he said warmly. "What a pleasant surprise. What brings you here?"

Hannah held up the basket, suddenly feeling foolish. "I... I baked some cookies. Thought your familye might enjoy them."

Eli's smile widened. "That's very kind of you. Would you like to come inside and drop them off? My mamm is putting some refreshments together for the women's circle."

Hannah hesitated, the overheard gossip still ringing in her ears. But the hopeful look in Eli's eyes made her resolve crumble. And... she didn't want *him* to overhear any of that talk, either.

"Jah, that would be nice."

As they walked towards the house, Eli's hand brushed against hers. The simple touch sent a jolt of energy zinging through her body. Her breathing stuttered for a moment though she disguised it by clearing her throat.

Hannah pulled away, guilt washing over her. What would Jacob think if he could see her now? Mary's words drifted through her mind.

...he wouldn't want you to be alone forever...

She inhaled through her nose and then exhaled through her mouth, slow and silent. Eli bounded up the front steps, holding the door open for her with a silly flourish. Hann ah smiled, heart lightening as she nodded her thanks and stepped over the threshold.

Inside, Sarah greeted them warmly, exclaiming over the cookies. As she bustled about making tea and putting a tray together for the women's group, Eli turned to Hannah.

"Would you like to take a walk?" he asked softly. "The orchard is beautiful this time of year."

Hannah nodded, unable to resist the warmth in his eyes. Her heart thumped, cheeks flushing as Sarah glanced at them, sidelong, a pleased smile on the older woman's lips.

With a start, Hannah realized Eli got his from his mamm. Though, given how infrequently his daed tended to smile, it was probably a good thing.

She followed him out the door, heading in the opposite direction from the gossips in the barn. He slowed his long stride to an amble, matching her speed so they walked side-by-side. As they strolled among the apple trees, a comfortable silence settled between them.

"Hannah," Eli began hesitantly. "Can I ask you something?"

She looked up at him, her heart racing. "Of course."

"Do you ever wonder... about Gott's plan for us?" Eli's voice was low, almost reverent. "About why things happen the way they do?"

Hannah's breath caught in her throat. "All the time," she admitted. "Especially since Jacob..."

Eli nodded understanding. "I've been thinking a lot about faith lately. About trusting in Gott's plan, even when we don't understand it."

"What do you mean?" Hannah asked, intrigued.

Eli's eyes met hers, intense and sincere. "I think... I think maybe Gott brought me back here for a reason. And maybe that reason is-"

"Eli!" The bishop's voice boomed across the orchard. "What are you doing all the way over there? There's work to be done!"

Hannah jumped back, suddenly aware of how close she and Eli had been standing. Samuel Zook approached at a quick walk, his expression stern.

"Bishop Zook," Hannah said politely, her cheeks flushing. "I was just dropping off some cookies."

Samuel's gaze softened slightly. He dipped his head at her. "That's very kind of you, Hannah. I am quite fond of your oatmeal ones. And..."

He cleared his throat, looking a little awkward as he broached the subject. "It's gut to see you out and about, not just in town at your shop. As you know we've all been praying for you and, ah, hoping for Gott to help you start to move on. It's what Jacob would have wanted."

Hannah froze, the words a bucket of cold water dousing her, soaking her to the skin. She shivered though the sun was warm on her face..

The bishop meant well. She knew that. He was a devout man, and kind in his way beneath his harsh exterior. However, his wife was the Zook who knew best how to handle delicate topics and conversations.

She knew the bishop meant well, but his words stung and she took a step back, automatically crossing her arms over her chest as if to ward off the reality of his words. He hadn't said anything different than Mary, but...

It didn't feel the same, coming from the bishop of their district.

"I... I should go," she stammered.

"Hannah, wait," Eli pleaded, reaching out toward her.

But Hannah was already backing away, her emotions in turmoil. "I'm sorry," she said, her voice barely above a whisper. She shook her head, slow at first then faster.

"This was a mistake. I'm not... I'm not ready for-for..." Her voice failed her. Hannah cleared her throat, not looking at him as she said, "I'm sorry, Eli. Gut day, Bishop."

As she hurried away, Hannah's back burned from the intensity of Eli's gaze. Tears stung her eyes. She'd just pushed away the one person who made her feel alive again.

Surely though, he wouldn't take the rejection too badly, right? She didn't mean forever, it was just... not time yet. Those careless words from earlier came back to her.

How do we even know he'll stay?

Hannah prayed Eli would keep waiting for her. If he didn't... well. Like that person from the women's circle had said-

She'll end up breaking her own heart at this rate.

Eli watched Hannah's retreating figure, his heart sinking. He'd been so close to telling her how he felt, and now... now she was running away from him.

This was a mistake...

Did she mean *Eli* was a mistake? Or just that the timing was a mistake? If all she needed was more time, Eli would wait.

He'd wait forever.

"Eli," Samuel's gruff voice broke through his thoughts. "I hope you're not getting any ideas about Hannh Stoltz-fus. She's might be coming out and about more, but she's still grieving. And right now? You are not a valid suitor for any woman in this community."

Eli turned to face his father, frustration bubbling up inside him. "Daed, with all due respect, you don't know what you're talking about. I'm trying to show you my commitment. I'm back and I'm not leaving. And Hannah is... she's special."

Samuel's eyebrows shot up. "Special? Sohn, you barely know her. You are different people now, both of you."

He frowned. "I pushed her too hard, perhaps, to move on in these recent months."

The bishop shot his son a hard look. "But as I said, she's not looking for any kind of relationship with someone like you. You'd do well to remember that."

As his father walked away, Eli clenched both of his hands into fists, glaring. Then, his shoulder slumped, despair washing over him.

Was his daed right? He'd thought Hannah might feel the same way he was. But her reaction to his father's words... the way she fled?

Maybe he'd been fooling himself all along.

Eli trudged back around the barn, his mind racing. Had he misread everything? Was Hannah just being kind to him out of pity? The memory of her soft smile, the way her eyes lit up when she saw him – it all seemed like a cruel joke now.

But Hannah wasn't cruel. Eli just... misunderstood her kindness in welcoming a prodigal son home.

As he threw himself into his work, Eli fought to push thoughts of Hannah from his mind. But with every swing of the axe, every bale of hay stacked, her face floated before him.

He'd never felt this way about anyone before, not here, and not in the Englisher world... now, it seemed he'd ruined everything before it even had a chance to begin. His mind whirled as he busied his hands with chores.

As the sun began to set, casting long shadows across the Zook property, Eli made a decision. He wouldn't let things end like this. He couldn't.

No, he *had* to talk to Hannah, had to explain himself and ask after her feelings for him, directly. Even if she didn't feel the same way, he needed her to know the truth and he had to hear the words from her mouth. For his own peace of mind.

Eli headed towards the house to clean up. He'd go to Hannah's home tonight, lay his heart bare. Whatever happened after that... well, he'd leave it in Gott's hands.

He played different scenarios through his mind as he washed up. Practiced a few stumbling, stuttering confessions, muttering them under his breath. Finally, he was ready.

But as he went downstairs, crossed the front room, and reached for the door to leave, he hesitated. His hand tightened on the doorknob.

What if Hannah *was* developing feelings but truly wasn't ready? What if pressing now only drove her further away, when patience might reward him beyond imagining?

Doubt crept in, paralyzing Eli. His hand fell away from the doorknob.

Maybe it was better to give Hannah space, to let her come to terms with her feelings on her own. But the thought of waiting, of not knowing, left his heart aching. He rubbed at his chest, then turned away and went back to his bedroom.

Later, as the full darkness of night fell over the Zook farm, Eli was still at that crossroads. Should he follow his heart and go to Hannah tomorrow after all? Or should he step back and wait until he'd proven himself further?

What was Gott's plan, His will for Eli? And... was he truly ready to accept His will, if it meant losing Hannah? Could he stay, and watch her find love with another?

Or was it better to just... leave it all behind a second time?

Chapter 8

A few weeks later, Eli sighed slightly as he hung the last of the decorative gourds along the community hall's rafters. He'd made trip after trip from the barn next door, used mostly for storage rather than being a working barn like on the many farms dotting the community.

The festive atmosphere of the Thanksgiving gathering was at odds with the knot of anxiety in his stomach. He could feel the weight of curious glances and hushed whispers following him as he moved about the room.

He hadn't spoken with Hannah once since that day in the orchard. Every time he thought about it, something told him to wait. And so, here he was, trusting in Gott even as his patience was tried just a little more, and ended up worn just a little bit thinner, with every passing day.

"Eli, could you help me with these tables?" John Lapp called out, struggling with a heavy folding table.

Grateful for the distraction, Eli hurried down the ladder and over to the other man. As they set up the table, John leaned in conspiratorially. "Don't let them get to you," he murmured. "You've been working harder than anyone since you got back. They'll come around."

Eli nodded, forcing a smile. "Danki, John. I appreciate that."

He wasn't so concerned with what most community members thought. They'd see his true character in time, his determination to stay. Eli cared about what Hannah thought, not others.

As more community members filtered in, the hall buzzed with excitement. Children darted between adults, their laughter a bright contrast to the undercurrent of tension across Eli's shoulders. He busied himself with last-minute preparations, determined to prove his worth through actions rather than words.

The creak of the main door caught his attention, and Eli's breath caught in his throat as Hannah entered with her family. Her eyes scanned the room, briefly meeting his before quickly looking away.

Eli's heart sank at the flash of uncertainty he saw there, but he steeled himself. Today wasn't about his feelings for Hannah.

It was about showing the community he was still here, still staying. That he belonged. First and foremost, convincing his daed, with one more day of commitment.

He'd stay the course, trust in Gott a little longer. If his path was by Hannah's side, Eli would find his way there.

But he still longed for that foggy uncertainty to lift, one way or another. Then, at least, he'd know for sure. At least he'd be out of this holding pattern.

His gaze darted back to Hannah after she'd passed by, and tracked her movements until she sat with her family.

As his daed took his place at the front of the room to begin the service, Eli found a spot near the back. He bowed his head in prayer, acutely aware of Hannah's presence just a few rows ahead and to one side.

Hannah nervously smoothed the fabric of her dress as she settled into her seat. He wasn't even that close, yet she could feel Eli's presence behind her, like a warm current in the air.

Part of her longed to turn and meet his gaze, to see if his eyes still held that spark of connection even after weeks of silence from her side. But she resisted, focusing instead on Bishop Samuel's words as he guided them through the lessons from scripture.

As the service progressed, Hannah found her mind wandering. She thought of Jacob, of the Thanksgivings and Christmases and all the years they'd planned to share but never would. The ache of his loss was still there, but it was softening a little, at long last.

Now, she felt a tentative hope, instead of that bleak, unending night. And when she'd caught a glimpse of Eli earlier, now weeks since that day in the orchard, her heart fluttered. Again.

She'd told the bishop she wasn't ready... and she wasn't. But would she ever truly feel ready?

Hannah was scared, and hadn't been praying on the situation with Eli. But... if she just trusted in Gott, He would never lead her astray.

"And let us be thankful for the return of those who have strayed. We welcome their return and, having found their way back, we pray for them to remain," Bishop Samuel's voice cut through her thoughts. His deep voice, usually so smooth and assured, hitched a little as he continued, adding, "For the prodigal sons and daughters who find their way back to Gott's embrace to recommit anew, baptized into new life."

Hannah shifted in her seat, automatically turning slightly until she could catch Eli's reaction from the corner of her eye. His jaw was set, his gaze fixed firmly ahead. She admired his strength in the face of such pointed words.

"Now, let us lift our voices in song."

As the congregation began to sing a hymn of thanks, Hannah's clear voice joined the others. For a moment, she allowed herself to imagine a future where she and Eli's voices blended in harmony, not just in song but in life.

It was terrifying, thinking about that future replacing the broken dreams she had with Jacob. But Jacob was gone, with the Lord now. Eli was right there.

She turned her head just a little more, almost catching his eye before she looked forward again.

That same future with Eli flashed through her mind, again.

This time, it was exhilarating.

Eli's voice faltered slightly as he caught Hannah's sideways glance. Even that brief moment of connection was enough to set his heart racing. But he forced himself to focus on the words of the hymn, on the gratitude he felt for this second chance.

After the song, and then the service, drew to a close, the sounds of chairs scraping against the floor filled the air. People chatted, mingling and moving towards the tables groaning under the weight of a veritable feast. Eli hung back, unsure of his place in the crowd.

"Did you hear about Eli Zook? Ach, not that he's *back*, that's old news," a hushed voice caught his attention. "No, I mean why. I heard he got into all sorts of trouble in the

English world. I don't think he's back for gut, no matter what the bishop says about prodigals."

"Shh," another voice admonished. "It's not our place to gossip. Besides, he seems to be trying hard to make amends. He's been working hard, you know."

The first voice scoffed, but didn't add anything.

Eli's cheeks burned as he gritted his teeth. Shame and frustration coiled in his chest like hissing snakes. He knew it would take time to regain the community's trust, but the constant scrutiny was wearing on him.

Especially without Hannah's gentle acceptance and encouragement to lean on.

Suddenly, a commotion near the door drew Eli's attention. And, a moment later, everyone else's, too.

"Fire!" a man shouted. "The barn's on fire!"

Gasps filled the air, men and women rushing and bumping into one another. Eli watched the panicked, milling crowd. Everyone was lost in the moment, disorganized.

In need of direction.

Without hesitation, Eli sprang into action. "Everyone stay calm," he called out, his voice carrying across the room.

"Men, follow me. We need to form a bucket brigade. Women, please take care of the children and elderly."

As he rushed towards the door, Eli caught Hannah's eye. He had no time to stop, but what he saw, a flash of admiration, a spark of the connection they'd shared, sent his resolve even higher.

Determination flooded his veins. He was focused on one thing: putting out the flames.

Chapter 9

Hannah's body thrummed with adrenaline as she watched Eli take charge. The authority in his voice, the confidence in his movements – it was a side of him she'd never seen before.

Not like this. For a moment, she forgot about the crisis at hand, mesmerized by the man Eli had become.

Shaking herself from her daze, Hannah turned to the women around her. "Let's get the kinner and the elderly to the far side of the hall," she said, her voice steady despite her inner turmoil, "and out of the way. Mary, can you gather blankets? Sarah, see if you can find any extra water or snacks."

As she helped guide people to safety, Hannah glanced out the window, her nostrils flaring as she inhaled sharply. The orange glow of the fire cast an eerie light across the gathering dusk. She could see Eli at the head of the bucket brigade, his strong arms passing buckets of water down the line, the precious liquid slopping over the rims.

"He's really stepped up," Mary murmured, appearing at Hannah's side. "Eli, I mean. Who would have thought?"

Hannah nodded, unable to tear her eyes away from the scene. "He's always had it in him," she said softly. "He just needed the chance to show everyone."

As the minutes ticked by, Hannah felt like she was working in tandem with Eli, despite the distance between them. When he called for more blankets to help smother smaller sparks, she was already sending them out. When she noticed some of the men looking exhausted, Eli was there with words of encouragement.

It was as if their old connection had resurfaced, stronger than ever. A warmth spread through Hannah, a light in her chest that had nothing to do with the nearby fire.

Instead, it was kindled by the man she watched through the window, spellbound.

Eli's muscles burned as he passed another bucket down the line. The acrid smell of smoke filled his nostrils, but he pushed through the discomfort. This was his chance to prove himself, to show the community that he was more than his past mistakes.

"We're gaining on it!" John Lapp shouted from further down the line. "Keep it up!"

Eli allowed himself a brief moment of hope. He glanced back towards the community hall, catching sight of Hannah coordinating efforts inside through the still-open doorway. Even through the smoke, he saw a quiet strength in her movements, a surety and grace under pressure.

A far cry from the bereaved widow who hardly left her shop.

As if sensing his gaze, Hannah looked up. Their eyes met across the chaos, and Eli felt a jolt of electricity that rivaled the nearby flames.

His feelings for her hadn't faded one bit. If anything, they'd grown stronger. He prayed they wouldn't leave him broken-hearted, not again.

"Eli!" His father's voice snapped him back to the present. "We need more water!"

Pushing thoughts of Hannah aside, Eli refocused on the task at hand. He organized a second line to the well, maximizing their efficiency. Time blurred as they battled the flames, each man working in tandem, every single one of them determined to defeat the fire.

Finally, after what felt like hours, but was more likely minutes, the last embers were extinguished. A ragged cheer went up from the men, lightness filling the still-smoky air. Eli sagged against the barn wall, scorched but intact, as exhaustion set in.

"Well done, son," Bishop Samuel said, approaching Eli. His voice was gruff, but there was a hint of pride in his eyes. "You showed real leadership out there."

Eli straightened, stunned by his father's words. "Danki, Daed," he managed. "I just did what needed to be done."

His father nodded, once, sharp but not dismissive like he'd been since Eli returned. The bishop turned to the crowd and raised his voice"We'll assess the damage later. For now, let us return to the hall."

As the sweaty, tired men made their way back to the community hall, Eli shifted on his feet. Was there some change in the atmosphere? He tensed, hearing whispers pick up again as he passed by.

But this time? The whispers that followed him were tinged with respect rather than suspicion. He allowed himself a small smile, grateful for this step towards redemption.

Grateful that Gott put Eli here, in this time and place, at just the moment he was needed. Grateful he got to help the community.

But most of all, grateful for whatever might come next with Hannah. She must have felt that same spark again. Right?

Hannah's heart swelled with pride as she watched Eli and the other men return. The quiet confidence in his bearing, the way the others looked to him with newfound respect – it was a sign of how quickly fickle opinions changed when faced with irrefutable evidence.

The evidence of his leadership and commitment. The evidence of how he'd grown from the shallow youth who left his community behind, but later returned, older and wiser.

As the community gathered once more, this time to offer prayers of gratitude for the mostly averted disaster, for if the fire had consumed the barn and community hall and maybe other buildings as well, it would have devastated their small district.

Hannah was drawn towards Eli, iron filings pulled inexorably, inevitably closer by a magnet. He was her lodestone. She weaved through the crowd, pausing just a few feet away from him.

"Let us bow our heads in thanks," Bishop Zook intoned. "For Gott's grace in protecting us from harm, and for the strength He gives us to face adversity together."

As Hannah bowed her head, she first sneaked a glance at Eli. His eyes were closed, his expression peaceful despite the soot smudged across his cheek.

Seeing him like this, now, after witnessing the depth of his character... Hannah's last reservations melted away. This was the man she'd always known Eli could be, even before he left – strong, compassionate, and deeply faithful.

When the silent prayer ended, a buzz of conversation filled the air. Hannah watched as person after person approached Eli, offering words of gratitude and praise. She hung back, letting the growing crowd push them farther apart, suddenly unsure of what to say.

Would he even *want* to talk to her? He had plenty of admirers and wellwishers now... and she'd run away from him.

"He did gut out there, didn't he?" Mary's voice startled Hannah from her thoughts.

"Jah, he did," Hannah agreed softly. "He's... he's really something. Everyone can see it, now."

Mary gave her a knowing look. "Ach, and how do *you* feel about that?"

She'd seen it earlier, believed in him before almost anyone else had... but had Hannah already lost her chance? Thrown it away out of fear?

Hannah opened her mouth to respond, but the words caught in her throat. How did she feel? The answer was both simple and terrifyingly complex.

Before she could verbalize a single word in reply, Eli looked over. Their eyes met across the crowded room.

Her mouth went dry. Her lungs tightened, as if the fire stole the oxygen from them despite being extinguished.

The intensity in his gaze, the questions that burned there – it was all too much and not enough at the same time.

She had to speak with him. Bare her heart and her soul and take a leap of faith. The time for hesitation and doubt was over.

Whatever lay ahead, she would trust in Gott to guide her through it, whether that meant a life with Eli in it, or heartbreak anew.

The community hall buzzed with activity as people helped clean up after the gathering, the excitement from the fire gradually settling into relieved conversations. Eli had just finished stacking the last of the chairs when his gaze caught Hannah's.

His heart pounded as the connection between them held, tension ratcheting up. The noise of the gathering faded away, leaving only the silent communication passing between them.

He saw the conflict in her eyes, but also a spark of something new – hope, perhaps? Or was it the same longing he felt in his own heart?

Or maybe, he was just fooling himself. But he was tired of waiting.

He took a step towards her, drawn by an invisible force. But before he could reach her, Bishop Samuel's hand landed heavily on his shoulder.

"Eli," his father said, his voice in an undertone for only his son's ears. "I think it's time we had a talk, when we get home. About your future here in the community."

Eli hesitated, torn between his duty to his father and his desire to speak with Hannah. He glanced back at her, seeing the flash of disappointment cross her face before she schooled her features into a polite smile.

"Of course, Daed," Eli replied, his voice steady despite the turmoil in his heart. "Whatever you think is best."

He glanced back at Hannah, but the moment was broken, another woman having captured her attention.

As he followed his father out of the hall, Eli exhaled a slow breath. He was at a crossroads, and soon, Gott willing, he'd follow the path he was always meant to live.

The events of the day shifted something fundamental in the community's perception of him. And maybe, more importantly, in Hannah's perception.

Whatever his father wanted to discuss, Eli knew one thing with certainty – he and Hannah would have a conversation of their own.

And soon.

The weight of unspoken words and suppressed feelings were too heavy for his heart to bear much longer. First, though.

First, he'd speak with his Daed. And then, with her parents.

As the cool night air hit his face, Eli sent up a silent prayer. For guidance, for courage, and for the strength to follow his heart, wherever it might lead.

Chapter 10

It was well past sunset by the time the Zooks returned home. Eli's muscles ached from the day's exertions, but his mind was alert, wondering what his father wanted to discuss. As they entered the house, the familiar scent of his mamm's bread lingered in the air, a comforting contrast to the acrid smell of smoke that still clung to their clothes.

Eli's heart pounded as he followed his father into the house. The evening air sent a shiver through his body, his skin still damp with sweat from fighting the fire. As they entered the kitchen, the familiar scent of his mamm's bread lingered in the air, a comforting contrast to the acrid smell of smoke that clung to his clothes.

Bishop Samuel turned to face his son, his expression unreadable. "Sit down, Eli," he said, gesturing to the kitchen table.

Eli lowered himself into a chair, his muscles aching from the day's exertion. He clasped his hands together to keep them from fidgeting, waiting for his father to speak.

The bishop sat across from him, his piercing gaze seeming to look right through Eli. "You showed real leadership out there today," he began, his voice gruff but not unkind.

"Danki, Daed," Eli replied softly. "I just did what needed to be done."

Samuel nodded slowly. "Jah, you did. And that's what I want to talk to you about." He paused, taking a deep breath. "You've changed, Eli. Since you've come back, I've seen you throw yourself into the work, into the community. You've shown a commitment I wasn't sure you still had in you."

Eli's throat tightened with emotion. "I meant what I said when I came back, Daed. This is where I belong. With our people, our faith."

"I see that now," Samuel admitted. "I'll be honest, when you first returned, I had my doubts. But you've proven yourself, time and again."

Hope bloomed in Eli's chest, but he remained silent, waiting for his father to continue.

"I've been watching you, Sohn. Not just your work on the farm, but how you've reconnected with the community. How you've been spending time with Hannah Stoltzfus."

Eli's cheeks warmed at the mention of Hannah's name. "Daed, I-"

Samuel held up a hand. "Let me finish. I've seen the way you look at her, Eli. And the way she looks at you." A ghost of a smile flickered across the bishop's face. "It reminds me of how your mamm and I were, all those years ago."

Eli's heart raced. Could his father truly be giving his blessing?

"You have my permission to court Hannah," Samuel said, his voice softening. "If that's what you want, and if her family agrees."

Joy surged through Eli, so intense he felt lightheaded. "Daed, I... danki. Truly."

Samuel nodded, then his expression grew serious once more. "But Eli, there's more we need to discuss. Your confession of faith, your baptism - these are important steps. You've shown your commitment, but there's still a path ahead of you."

"I understand," Eli said earnestly. "I'm ready, Daed. I want to fully rejoin the church, to make my commitment before Gott and the community."

"Gut," Samuel replied. "We'll talk more about this in the coming days. There's much to prepare."

Throat tight, Eli stood, overwhelmed with gratitude and hope. Then, his father surprised him by pulling him into a brief, tight embrace.

"I'm proud of you, Sohn," Samuel murmured. "Welcome home."

Eli blinked back tears as he returned the embrace. "Danki, Daed," he whispered. "I won't let you know, I promise."

As he left the house a little while later for a walk, stepping out into the cool evening air, Eli's heart was lighter than it had been in years. He sent up a silent prayer of thanks to Gott for guiding him home, for this second chance.

And for Hannah. Sweet, beautiful Hannah. He couldn't wait to see her, to ask her to court. With a smile on his face and joy in his heart, Eli set off with quick steps. He ought to practice, before going to see her parents.

The following week, after many long conversations with his daed and no time at all to so much as drive or walk by Hannah's quilt to catch a glimpse of her, Eli was ready.

It was time he asked Hannah's parents for their permission and blessing to court their daughter. And so, he'd driven his buggy to the King family farm.

Now, his palms sweating, heart pounding with anxious tension, he stood before Hannah's parents, his palms sweating despite the chill in the early December air. He'd rehearsed this moment a hundred times in his mind, but now that it was here, words seemed to fail him.

"Mr. and Mrs. King," he began, his voice shakier than he'd like. "I've come to ask your permission to court your daughter, Hannah."

The silence that followed seemed to stretch for an eternity. Eli forced himself to meet their eyes, praying they could see the sincerity in his heart.

Finally, Mr. King spoke. "Eli Zook, you've certainly proven yourself these past months. But Hannah... she's been through so much. Losing Jacob," he shook his head.

"I know, sir," Eli said earnestly. "And I would never push her before she's ready. I just... I care for her deeply, and I'd like the chance to show her - and you - that my intentions are honorable. I-I've spoken to my daed quite frequently this last week. He's accepted my confession of faith and granted his blessing to come ask you today."

He saw them exchange a glance and hurried to add, "My baptism will be quite soon, perhaps before Christmas, Gott willing. I am committed to this life, and I am committed to Hannah, if she'll have me," he said, voice firm. He didn't want them to doubt his intentions one bit.

Mrs. King reached for her husband's hand, a small smile playing on her lips. "I think Hannah has been ready for some time now," she said softly. "But scared, in many ways, to open up again. But we've seen how she lights up around *you*, Eli."

Eli's heart soared at her words. "So, does that mean...?"

Mr. King nodded slowly. "Jah, Eli Zook. You have our permission to ask Hannah to court. But," he added, his tone growing serious, "you treat her with the utmost respect. She's precious to us. And you, young man, are not officially baptized yet."

"Of course, sir," Eli agreed quickly. "I'll honor her in every way."

As he left the King home, Eli couldn't keep the grin off his face. He had permission to court Hannah. Now, he just needed to plan the perfect first outing.

Oh, but first?

He had to ask Hannah if she even wanted to court...

Chapter 11

E li's mouth went dry as he pushed open the door to Hannah's quilt shop, the little bell hanging above ringing as cheerful as ever. The scent of freshly pressed fabric and lavender sachet enveloped him, reminding him of his mamm's sewing room. His eyes scanned the colorful bolts of fabric lining the walls before finally settling on Hannah herself.

"Gut afternoon, Eli," Hannah's soft voice called out from behind the counter. "I-it's nice to see you again. Can I help you with something?"

Eli's heart skipped a beat as he turned to face her. Hannah's warm hazel eyes met his, a gentle smile playing on her lips. He swallowed hard, suddenly aware of how important this moment was. This... this would make or break his future... and his heart.

"Hannah," he began, his voice a touch shakier than he'd like. "I was hoping we could talk for a moment. If you're not too busy, that is."

Hannah's brow furrowed slightly, but her smile remained. "Of course, Eli. Let me just..."

She glanced around the empty shop, then called out, "Mary? Would you mind watching the front for a few minutes?"

Mary appeared from the back room, a knowing smile blooming bright on her face when her gaze landed on Eli. "Certainly, Hannah. Take your time."

Eli's neck heated as Mary winked at him before bustling behind the counter, swapping places with her friend. He followed Hannah to a quiet corner of the shop, his palms sweating.

"Are-are you well, Eli?" Hannah asked, her voice a little stilted, hesitant.

He didn't let himself wonder why. Right now, he had a question to ask.

"Jah, everything is... well, it's wonderful, actually," Eli said, gathering his courage. "My daed and I have been speaking about my baptism and officially joining the community. And, Hannah, I-I, well."

He cleared his throat, rubbing at the back of his neck. Eli forced himself to meet her gaze as he said, "I've just come from speaking with your parents."

Hannah's eyes widened, lips parting slightly as surprise and something else, an emotion he prayed was hope, flickered across her face. "Oh?"

Eli took a deep breath, then after a quick glance around to make sure no one was there, boldly reached out to gently take Hannah's hands in his. He cheered internally when she let him, her fingers darting down, looking at their hands in shock as a bright, almost disbelieving smile lit her pretty features.

"Hannah Stoltzfus, I care for you deeply. These past months since my return, I've had many blessings, too many to count. But getting to know you again, seeing your kindness, your strength, your faith... that has been the greatest blessing of all. Perhaps the greatest blessing of my life"

He could feel Hannah's hands trembling slightly in his. Or perhaps it was his own hands that shook?

"With your parents' blessing, and if you're willing, I would be honored to court you, properly," he said in a rush.

Hannah's breath caught, her eyes blinking, a sheen of moisture rising to brighten her gaze even more than usual. "Oh, Eli," she whispered.

For one horrible, stomach-churning moment, he feared all was lost. That moment, longer than an eternity, left Eli's heart hanging in suspense, stealing the breath from his lungs.

Then, all at once, a radiant smile spread across Hannah's face.

"Jah, Eli," she said, her voice full of emotion. "I would be honored to court you."

Joy surged through Eli's body, so intense he felt he might burst. Without thinking, he pulled Hannah into a brief, tight embrace, wholly unmindful of the shop's open setting and Mary's presence nearby.

As they separated, both blushing furiously but unable to stop smiling, Eli said softly, "Danki, Hannah. You've made me the happiest man in the world."

Hannah ducked her head shyly, but her eyes shone with happiness when she looked back up at him. "And you've made me very happy too, Eli Zook."

From across the shop, Mary called out, "I think this calls for a celebration! I'll close up early and we can all have some coffee and cookies."

Eli and Hannah laughed, the sound of their joy mingling in the air. Mary bustled about, studiously *not* looking at the couple as she turned the sign from *Open* to *Closed*, then hummed on her way to the back where she'd prepare the treats.

Eli gazed at Hannah, marveling at this amazing woman who chose to walk this path Gott had led them to. With Hannah by his side and Gott guiding their way, Eli could face anything. The future stretched out before him, bright with promise and love.

Hannah's fingers trembled as she smoothed her dress, peering out the window for the hundredth time. The freshly fallen snow sparkled in the late afternoon sun, turning the world into a winter wonderland.

But Hannah barely noticed its beauty. Her mind was filled with thoughts of Eli and their first official outing as a courting couple. He'd asked almost immediately after leaving her parents' home with their blessing, rushing into her shop in a whirlwind of nerves and bright hope.

And now, here she was. At her parents' home, waiting for her beau to arrive. It was similar, yet so very different from when Jacob courted her...

"You look lovely, dear," her mother said, appearing at her side. "Stop fussing. Eli will be here any minute."

As if on cue, the sound of horse hooves filled the air. Hannah's heart leaped as she caught sight of Eli guiding a large, horse-drawn buggy up their lane, wheels creaking over the packed-down snow.

He looked so handsome, his cheeks ruddy from the cold, a bright smile lighting up his face. That same bright smile as when she'd bashfully accepted his courtship.

"Remember, Mary and John will be chaperoning," her father reminded her as she reached for her coat. "And be home by eight."

"Jah, Daed," Hannah promised, trying to keep the excitement from her voice. "We'll be careful."

As she stepped outside, Eli jumped down from the buggy to help her in. His strong hand gripped tight for a moment as he helped her up into the vehicle. The brief contact sent a jolt of electricity through her body, even through their thick gloves.

"You look beautiful," Eli murmured, his eyes never leaving hers.

Hannah's cheeks warmed, and not just from the cold. "Danki," she managed. "You look very handsome yourself."

Mary and John were already seated at the back of the sleigh, their presence a gentle reminder of propriety. But as Eli urged the horse forward, Hannah couldn't help but feel like they were in a world of their own.

The wheels rolled over the snow-covered roads, as the soft crunch of snow beneath them offered a crisp soundscape. Hannah snuck glances at Eli, admiring the way he handled the reins with such confidence.

"I can't believe this is really happening," Eli said softly, his words meant only for her ears. "I've dreamed of this moment for so long."

Hannah's heart swelled with emotion. "Jah, me too," she admitted. "I was so afraid to let myself feel this way again. T-to even consider moving on. But with you... it just feels right."

Eli's smile was radiant. "I promise you, Hannah, I'll do everything in my power to make you happy."

As they rode through the countryside, a serene peace settled over Hannah, like a blanket of fresh snow, softening the landscape and bringing a hush of quiet to the world.

The guilt that plagued her for so long melted away like snow in the spring sun. This, she realized, was exactly where she was meant to be.

It was where Jacob would want her to be. Happy and content at last.

Chapter 12

Eli didn't even try to keep the broad smile off his face as he guided the buggy back towards Hannah's home. The afternoon was perfect - filled with laughter, shared stories, and stolen glances. Even with Mary and John chaperoning, Eli had felt a deepening connection with Hannah.

As they approached the King family's farm, Eli slowed the horse. He wasn't ready for their time together to end. But come to an end, it must.

"Hannah," he said softly, "I know it's only our first courtship outing, but I want, no I *need* to make sure you know... I've never felt this way about anyone before. Not in our district, not in the English word. It's only ever been you. And with you, everything just feels... right."

Hannah's eyes shone in the fading light. "Oh, Eli," she breathed. "I-I feel that rightness, too. I think," she said lowly, "I think that wa spart of the problem, for me. I love Jacob still, I always will. But what I feel for you? It's almost terrifying, how right this feels."

Eli longed to take her hand, to pull her close in his embrace. To press a soft kiss to her brow, her cheeks.. Her lips.

But he was acutely aware of Mary and John's presence behind them. Instead, he poured all his emotion into his gaze, willing Hannah to understand the depth of his feelings.

"I know we have to take things slow," he said. "I-I'm not even baptized yet. But I want you to know that I'm committed to this - to us. Whatever comes, we'll face it together."

Hannah nodded, her smile radiant. "Together," she agreed.

As they pulled up to the house, Eli helped Hannah down from the buggy. Their hands lingered together for a moment, clasped tight for longer than necessary, neither wanting to let go.

"Gut night, Hannah," Eli said, his voice low. "I'll see you tomorrow at the Bible study?"

"Jah," Hannah replied, cheeks pink. From the cold? Or something else? "I'm looking forward to it," she said with a soft smile, a dimple forming in one cheek.

Watching her disappear into the house with a final wave of farewell, Eli sighed. His cheeks hurt from grinning so much and his heart raced.

Joy and longing bloomed in his ribcage in equal measure. Tomorrow.

He'd get to see Hannah again tomorrow. He could wait that long.

Probably, anyway.

ell

Hannah's heart was still racing as she closed the door behind her. A giddy smile refused to leave her face. The memory of Eli's brief touch as he helped her on and off the buggy... his earnest words...

It all filled her with a warmth that had nothing to do with the cozy fire blazing in the hearth.

"How was your buggy ride?" her mother asked, a knowing smile on her face.

"It was... wonderful," Hannah admitted, unable to keep the joy from her voice. "Eli is so kind and thoughtful. And he makes me laugh, Mamm. I-I'd forgotten how gut that feels."

Her mother's eyes softened. "I'm so happy for you, Hannah. You deserve this joy."

As Hannah prepared for bed that night, her mind whirled with thoughts of Eli. She was looking forward to the Bible study tomorrow, eager to see him again. But a small tendril of that same nagging guilt crept into her heart.

Was it wrong to feel this happy, this excited about a new relationship?

She kneeled by her bedside, closing her eyes and clasping her hands in prayer. "Dear Lord," she whispered, "please guide my heart. Help me to honor Jacob's memory while embracing this new chapter You've given me. And Gott... thank You, so very much, for Eli."

For long minutes, she stayed like that, patient as she petitioned for His help. A little while later, she felt an ease fill her chest.

As she climbed into bed, Hannah relaxed, the guilt melting away. Gott's blessing rested in her heart and she let the sense of peace wash over her. Whatever lay ahead, she knew that with Gott's guidance and Eli by her side, she would face and persevere.

The next evening, Eli sat next to Hannah at the Bible study for the community's young folk. The warmth of her presence beside him made it difficult to focus on the scripture being discussed.

He glanced sideways at her constantly, as if he was a compass and Hannah was true north. Sometimes, she was already looking back at him. And every time their eyes met, Eli's heart skipped, then sped up. The cycle repeated itself during the entire session.

As the group delved into a passage about love and forgiveness, Eli instantly saw the parallels to his own journey. He'd returned home seeking redemption, and instead, he'd found so much more. He'd found belonging, love... and Hannah.

"What do you think, Eli?" the group leader asked, startling him from his thoughts. "How does this passage apply to our daily lives?"

Eli cleared his throat, acutely aware of Hannah's gaze on him. "Well," he began, "I think it reminds us that Gott's love is unconditional. Just as He forgives us, we should strive to forgive others - and ourselves. It's about second chances and new beginnings."

He felt Hannah's sleeve brush against his, a silent gesture of support. Eli's heart swelled with gratitude for her understanding, her acceptance of his past.

As the study concluded, Eli and Hannah lingered, neither eager to part ways.

"That was a beautiful interpretation," Hannah said softly. "You have a deep understanding of scripture."

Eli ducked his head, humbled by her praise. "I've had a lot of time to reflect on Gott's word," he admitted. "It's been a source of comfort and guidance, especially since coming home. And with my daed," he paused and chuckled. "Well, 'Just the basics,' he said, but I think he's determined I"ll know it inside and out before my baptism."

Hannah's eyes shone with warmth. "I'm so glad you did come home, Eli. I can't imagine my life without you in it now."

Eli longed to pull her close, to express the depth of his feelings. But surrounded by community members, he settled for a gentle smile.

"I feel the same way, Hannah. You've brought so much light into my life," he murmured. "More than I ever thought existed in the whole wide world."

She ducked her head, smiling.

As they parted ways that evening, Eli felt purpose filling his soul. He knew now, more than ever, that Hannah was the one he wanted to build a future with. And he was determined to prove himself worthy of her love.

First, he needed his daed to have no doubts before Eli's upcoming baptism. So he'd better get back home and keep studying the scriptures.

Chapter 13

The weeks leading up to Christmas flew by in a whirlwind of activity. Eli's baptism took place earlier in the month, her beau having succeeded in showing his commitment to the faith and their community, even to his father's stringent, extremely high standards.

The bishop held Eli to even higher standards than average, perhaps because he didn't want any accusations of favoritism, or perhaps because of Eli's years in the English world. Either way, Eli Zook rose to the occasion, as she knew he would.

And now, Hannah was busier than ever, splitting her time between her work at the quilt shop and community preparations for the holiday.

Not to mention continuing her beautiful courtship with Eli. No matter how hectic things got, she always found moments to spend with him, and he with her. Even if it meant he came to her shop to eat in the middle of the day, snatching half an hour in their days, the pair made time for each other.

For their future.

One frosty December afternoon, Hannah joined the other women in the community hall, preparing food for the upcoming Christmas feast. As she kneaded dough for bread, her gaze was pulled, again and again, to where Eli worked outside, helping the other men hang festive garlands on the fully repaired barn.

"You're going to wear out that window if you keep staring at it," Mary teased, nudging Hannah's shoulder.

Hannah felt her cheeks flush. "I wasn't staring," she protested weakly.

Mary's knowing smile said it all. "Ach, you were. But it's nee bad thing. It's gut to see you so happy, Hannah. You're practically glowing these days."

Hannah ducked her head, focusing on the dough beneath her hands. "I am happy," she admitted softly. "Eli... he's everything I never knew I needed. But sometimes I still worry..."

She frowned, kneading the dough with extra force. These silly doubts refused to leave her for good, springing up like weeds every few days despite the surety her prayers gave her that this was the path Gott meant for her, and for Eli, to follow. Together.

"About what?" Mary prompted gently.

"That it's still somehow too soon. That I'm not honoring Jacob's memory like I ought, feeling this way about Eli. About our future together."

Mary's expression softened. "Oh, Hannah. Do you really think Jacob would want you to spend the rest of your life alone? He loved you. He'd want you to be happy. I've told you this before," she said, lightly scolding with mock sternness.

Hannah blinked as tears prickled at her eyes. "I know you're right. It's just... sometimes the guilt still creeps in."

"That's natural," Mary assured her. "It will fade all the way in time. Just don't let it hold you back from embracing this new chapter. You deserve love and happiness, Hannah. And from what I've seen, Eli is a gut man who truly cares for you. And he needs you too, you know. You'll find that love and happiness together, the both of you. "

Hannah nodded, weight lifting from her shoulders. "Danki, Mary. I don't know what I'd do without your friendship and wisdom."

As they returned to their work, Hannah's eyes drifted once more to the window. This time, she caught Eli looking her way.

He flashed her a warm smile that made her heart skip a beat. Mary was right.

She smiled back, giving a shy wave. It was time to fully embrace this new love, without guilt or reservation.

Christmas morning dawned bright and clear, a fresh blanket of snow covering the world in pristine white. Eli hurried through his chores, eager to see Hannah. They'd agreed to exchange small gifts after the community gathering, and he couldn't wait to give her the present he'd spent weeks crafting.

As he made his way to the King family farm, Hannah's gift tucked securely under his arm, Eli's mind wandered to the future.

He'd been thinking a lot about the next step in their relationship, about making their engagement official in the eyes of the community. But was it too soon? He'd only been baptized a few weeks ago.

And... was Hannah ready for that new level to their relationship already? Oh, he knew she was committed to their future, but that didn't mean she was already prepared for the next step yet.

Hannah greeted him at the door, her smile as warm as the sun on snow. "Frohe Weihnachten, Eli," she said softly.

"Frohe Weihnachten, Hannah," he replied, drinking in the sight of her. Even in her simple dress and kapp, she was the most beautiful woman he'd ever seen. And not only that, but every time he saw her, she grew even more beautiful to him.

They settled in the parlor, acutely aware of Hannah's parents' presence in the next room. Eli handed Hannah his gift, suddenly nervous. "I hope you like it," he said, rubbing one hand at the back of his neck.

Hannah carefully unwrapped the package, untying the twine and pulling the brown paper away. She gasped softly as she revealed a beautifully carved wooden box. Simple, yet beautiful patterns of vines adorned the lid, each detail lovingly crafted by Eli's hands. He'd made a few false starts at first, but eventually got the hang of carving back by sheer grit and will alone.

"Oh, Eli," Hannah breathed. "It's beautiful. Did you make this yourself?"

Eli nodded, warmth spreading through his chest at her reaction. "I thought you could use it for your sewing notions," he explained. "I know how much your work means to you."

Hannah's eyes shone with emotion. "It's perfect. Danki, Eli. Truly."

She handed him a package of her own, wrapped in simple brown paper just like her gift's wrappings. Eli opened it carefully, revealing a hand-knit scarf in a deep, rich blue.

"Hannah, this is wonderful," he said, running his fingers over the soft wool. He swiftly wrapped it around his neck, tucking his chin into the warm fibers and inhaling.

Eli looked at Hannah, the corners of his eyes crinkling as he said, "I'll think of you every time I wear it."

Their eyes met, and the rest of the world faded away. Eli swallowed hard. He wanted nothing more than to take his love into his arms and keep her safe, forever. But this was not the time, nor place. Not yet.

Instead, he contented himself with a crooked smile, pouring all his love into his gaze as he stared into her eyes.

"Hannah," he said softly, "I was wondering if you'd like to go on somewhere special with me next week. There's something important I'd like to discuss with you."

Hannah's eyes widened slightly, excitement warring with nervousness on her pretty features. "Of course, Eli. I'd love to."

"Gut," he said, beaming. "Danki, Hannah."

Soon, her parents said it was nearly suppertime. Eli took his leave, though they invited him to stay. While his daed seemed like he was the strict parent, Eli knew full well the sort of lecture waiting for him should he miss Christmas supper at their home.

And so, Eli left the King home that evening, his heart full of hope and anticipation. He had a plan in his mind - a plan that would change both their lives forever. All he needed now was to take that final step.

The days between Christmas and New Year's were passing by in a blur for Hannah. Her mind was consumed with thoughts of Eli and the "important discussion" he'd mentioned.

Could it be? Was he planning to ask her to marry him?

The day of their outing dawned bright and cold and clear. As she readied in the morning, Hannah paused before going downstairs.

By the end of the day, she might be an engaged woman for the second time.

"Jacob," she murmured, brushing her fingertips over the keepsake box with flowers. "I'm finally happy again. I'm so grateful for our time together, and I will always remember our love. It's time for me to move on. Eli is a gut man. You'd like him, I think."

Then, she touched the lid of the second box beside it. Her Christmas gift from Eli, covered in twining vines. It went nicely with the flower-carved box from Jacob.

She smiled, exhaling a happy sigh and left the room.

As she walked downstairs, Hannah was filled with a peace she never would have expected to find every again. Not after losing Jacob.

But Eli's return brought more than just a son home at last. It led to a new love for Hannah, a bright new future she hoped would be even brighter, after today.

And the guilt that had plagued her for so long was quiet, melted away since seeing Eli on Christmas Day. Instead, in its place was a quiet certainty that this was right. That Eli was right for her and she for him.

Hannah checked the ticking clock on the mantle. It was nearly time for Eli's arrival. She sucked in a breath, then blew it out quickly.

The young woman patted her kapp and smoothed her skirts down before reaching for her scarf, a slightly lighter blue than the one she'd made and gifted to Eli. She wound it snugly around her neck, the reached for her overcoat. Her gloves, the same shade of blue as her scarf, peeked from the front pocket.

"You look lovely," her mother said, helping her fasten her coat. "Are you nervous?"

Hannah shook her head, surprised to find it was true. "Nee, Mamm. I'm... excited. Whatever Eli wants to discuss, I know it's part of Gott's plan for us."

Her mother's eyes filled with tears. "Oh, my sweet girl. I'm so happy for you. Jacob would be too, you know. He'd want you to find love again."

Hannah hugged her mother tightly, grateful for her understanding and support. "Danki, Mamm. That means more than you know."

As Eli's buggy pulled up outside, Hannah's chest fluttered with anticipation, like a cloud of butterflies taking flight into the sunset. She opened the door and stepped out, eager to see him. Eager to begin the rest of her life - with Eli by her side and Gott guiding their path.

Chapter 14

Eli's heart pounded as he helped Hannah down from the buggy, his gloved hand lingering in hers a moment longer than necessary. Mary and John rode with them to chaperone, but with a wink, Hannah's friend had loudly said she'd rather stay in the buggy, with the propane heater.

Her husband only laughed, and said, "You're just going to the creek, jah?"

Eli nodded and now he and Hannah were walking side by side through the cold air, crisp snow crunching under their feet. He took a deep breath, watching the cold frost curl up in front of him when he exhaled.

The frozen creek stretched before them, a shimmering ribbon under the bright sun, sparkling in the winter landscape. He could hardly believe they were here again, in the very spot where they, along with all the other kinner from the community, spent countless hours during those long-ago childhood winters sliding across the ice.

"Oh, Eli," Hannah breathed, her eyes sparkling. "It's just like I remember. Look at how the ice glistens in the sunlight!"

Eli nodded, drinking in her excitement. "Jah, it's beautiful. Almost as beautiful as you," he added softly. He was warm despite the cold, just from his love's presence beside him.

Hannah ducked her head, pressing gloved hands to her cheeks. He could still see the becoming blush spreading across her face, though how much was form his words and how much was from the air nipping at their skin, he couldn't say.

"You're such a charmer, Eli Zook," she said in an amused tone.

As they made their way to the creek's edge, Eli was acutely aware of their chaperones still in plain view, though watching from a growing distance in the buggy. He appreciated their presence; it kept him anchored when all he wanted was to sweep Hannah into his arms and never let go.

"Remember how we used to race from the big oak to the next bend in the creek?" Hannah asked, her voice tinged with nostalgia.

Eli grinned. "Jah, and you always won, somehow. Everyone else ended up slipping and sliding, going down in a tangle on the ice."

"Are you saying I cheated?" Hannah teased, her eyes dancing with mirth.

"Never," Eli replied solemnly, though his lips twitched with suppressed laughter. "I was simply admiring your natural talents."

Hannah's laughter rang out, clear and bright in the crisp air. Eli's heart swelled at the sound. This was it - the moment he'd been waiting for.

"Hannah," he began, taking her gloved hands in his. "There's something I want to ask you."

Her bright gaze stared up at him, expectant. She must know what he was going to ask, yet what if the answer wasn't what he'd hoped, prayed for every night since she'd accepted his courtship?

Hannah's breath caught in her throat as Eli's deep blue eyes met hers. There was an intensity in his gaze that made her heart race. She knew what was coming next.

They'd agreed to court, after all, and everyone knew the intended outcome of courtship was marriage. If he wasn't committed to building a future with her, he would never have even asked to court.

But still, it was different, being in this moment.

"Jah, Eli?" she managed, her voice barely above a whisper.

Eli took a deep breath, his hands tightening around hers. "Hannah Stoltzfus, when I came back to Lancaster County, I never imagined I'd find something so precious. You've brought light back into my life, shown me what it means to truly love and be loved in return."

Tears pricked at Hannah's eyes as Eli continued, his voice thick with emotion.

"I know we've both faced challenges, but with you by my side, I feel like I can overcome anything. You make me want to be a better man - for you, for our community, and for Gott."

Hannah's heart soared as Eli slowly reached into his heavy winter coat, pulling a small box from his pocket.

"Hannah, my love, would you do me the incredible honor of becoming my wife? Will you build a life with me, raise a familye together, and grow old by my side?" he asked, voice somber, yet his eyes were lit with joy. Joy, and so much love she was overwhelmed.

For a moment, Hannah couldn't speak. Pure happiness bubbled up inside her, threatening to overflow. A bright smile stretched across her face, so big her cheeks hurt, as she blinked back tears.

He still held out the box, and she took it with trembling hands. It was smaller than the one from Christmas, but clearly carved to be a matched pair. She opened it, and inside she found a carved wooden heart, with their first initials intertwined.

"It's not quite traditional," he said, sounding a little sheepish. "But... you have my heart, always. I-I hope that's all right."

She looked up at Eli, his face so full of hope and love. Of course, there was only one answer she could give. The answer he must know was inevitable, yet he'd brought her here to ask her, just the two of them.

"I'll take gut care of it," she said, voice just above a whisper. "As long as you take care of mine, too."

He smiled and nodded. "Jah, of course." Eli shifted on his feet, still smiling but looking a little more nervous. "Does that mean you accept?" he asked. Hannah laughed, the sound a little wet but full of love. "Ach, of course I do. Jah, Eli," she said, tears of happiness spilling down her cheeks. "A thousand times over. There's nothing I want more than to be your fraa."

Eli's face broke into a radiant smile as he took half a step closer to her. Heedless of their audience, he pulled her into an embrace.

She wrapped her arms around him, clutching tight at his strong back. Mary and John wouldn't take issue with a simple hug, she was certain.

"I love you, Hannah," he murmured against her hair. "More than I ever thought possible."

"And I love you, Eli," Hannah replied, her voice filled with warmth. "With all my heart."

How long they stood like that, embracing and luxuriating in the joyous moment, only Gott knew. Well, Gott, as well as Mary and John Lapp.

Finally, a shiver went through her body, winter's merciless grip making itself known. Eli pulled back, and said, "Ach, you must be freezing. Let's get back to the buggy. I'm sure Mary still has the heater going."

Hannah nodded and smiled up at him. They untangled from their embrace, but walked very close back to the buggy.

Hannah clutched the little box in her hand, the secret heart inside only known to her and to Eli and to Gott. She'd keep his heart safe, and trust him with hers for the rest of their lives.

Chapter 15

The next few months of winter passed in a whirlwind of preparations and anticipation. Eli threw himself into his work on the Zook farm, determined to provide a solid foundation for his future with Hannah by preparing for the coming spring and years to come. Every spare moment was spent either with her or thinking of her, his heart full to bursting with love and gratitude.

As the first signs of spring appeared, from birdsong to longer and longer hours of daylight, warming temperatures and melting snow, the day of their wedding drew closer and closer. Neither of them wanted to wait until the traditional fall harvest to marry. And, given Eli's intense study of scripture, his daed finally relented and agreed to let them move the wedding up into springtime, after the first planting was completed.

Now, Eli stood before the single, full-length mirror in his childhood home, adjusting his collar for what felt like the hundredth time. Today was the long-awaited day at last - the day he'd marry Hannah before Gott and their entire community.

"You look fine, son." His father's deep voice came from the doorway. "Stop fussing."

Eli turned, surprised to see a slight sheen in the older man's eyes. Right now, he wasn't the stern Bishop Zook, but Samuel, husband and proud father.

"Daed," he said softly. "I didn't hear you come in."

Samuel crossed the room, placing a hand on Eli's shoulder. "I'm proud of you, Eli. The man you've become... the way you've embraced our way of life again..."

He cleared his throat, squeezing his son's shoulder. "It's everything I prayed for but didn't really believe would happen, sometimes. Your mamm never lost her faith in you, but I-I struggled over the years, daring to hope for all of this. Gott truly is great," he finished gruffly.

Eli felt a lump form in his throat. "Danki, Daed. That means more to me than you know."

For a moment, father and son stood in silence, years of misunderstanding and hurt melting away in the face of this new beginning.

"Well," Samuel finally said, clearing his throat. "We'd better get going. Can't keep your bride waiting, can we?"

Eli nodded, taking one last look in the mirror. This was it - the start of his new life with Hannah. As he followed his father out of the room, Eli sent up a silent prayer of thanks for the path he'd been led to follow. Even when he'd lost his way, Gott was always there waiting to guide him back.

Back to his home, his family, his faith.

Back to Hannah and a love he never imagined.

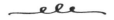

Hannah smiled as she smoothed the fabric of her wedding dress. The simple blue dress she'd made reflected her Amish values of modesty and simplicity.

But as Hannah caught sight of her reflection, she felt utterly, completely beautiful. A light shone from within, the love in her heart reflected in her eyes and on her face, though she only wore a slight smile at the moment. Gott's love and blessings rained down on her, and today, she and Eli would begin their life together.

"Oh, Hannah," her mother breathed, tears glistening in her eyes. "You look absolutely radiant, so happy. It's gut to see."

Hannah turned, embracing her mother tightly. "Danki, Mamm. For everything. I couldn't have asked for a better example of love and faith."

As her cousins bustled around, making last-minute adjustments, Hannah's gaze fell on the wedding quilt draped over a nearby chair, with the double wedding ring pattern partially visible.

She'd poured her heart and soul into every stitch, each square telling a part of her and Eli's story. There were moments when the task had felt overwhelming, especially when they moved the wedding date up, but now, seeing it complete, Hannah felt a sense of peace wash over her.

"It's time," her father's gentle voice called from the doorway. "Are you ready, mein dochder?"

Hannah took a deep breath, smoothing her apron one last time. "Jah, Daed. I'm ready."

As she took her father's arm, Hannah's stomach flipped with a little flutter of nerves. But it wasn't fear or doubt - it was pure, joyful anticipation.

In just a little while, she would be walking into the community hall to meet Eli, the man who captured her heart and showed her that love could bloom again. Losing Jacob was devastating, and this new chance at love with Eli was the most amazing blessing she never expected.

The scent of freshly turned dirt and spring mingled in the air, wildflowers and new greenery creating a rustic perfume that perfectly captured the essence of their Amish community as her daed drove their buggy into town.

As they approached the open doorway, the familiar melody of voices singing filled the air as Hannah and her father made their way to the barn where the ceremony would take place.

And then, there he was. Eli stood at the front of the gathering, his eyes fixed on Hannah with such love and adoration it took her breath away. Beside Eli, Bishop Zook stood tall and serene.

But she only had eyes for her future husband. As she walked towards Eli, Hannah's smile grew and grew as her heart pounded.

This was it. The start of their new life together. A bright future that brought her such joy, she feared she might burst from happiness.

She couldn't tear her gaze from his, though she knew their community was in full attendance to witness this special day. Finally, she took the final few steps and stopped beside Eli, giving him a blinding smile as tears of happiness welled in her eyes.

Eli watched with rapt attention as Hannah walked down the aisle towards him. She was a vision in a new, neat blue dress, her face glowing with joy and love. All of Eli's lingering doubts and fears melted away like the winter's snow melting before the returning sun.

This was right. This was meant to be. Gott led them both to walk this path together, to build a new life and a new family.

As Hannah reached his side, Eli's hand twitched, as he yearned to take her hand in his. Instead, he clasped his hands and simply remembered how on their courtship outings he'd had that privilege. How he'd marveled at how perfectly their hands fit together. How he'd have the chance to do so again soon enough.

His father's voice rang out, beginning the ceremony, but Eli could barely focus on the words. All he could see was Hannah, all he could feel was the phantom warmth of her hand in his, a lingering memory he wanted to recreate over and over again, for the rest of their lives.

Bishop Samuel Zook stood before the congregation, his voice carrying across the simple meetinghouse. "Today, we gather to witness Eli and Hannah join their lives in holy matrimony before Gott and this community."

Eli's eyes met Hannah's, his heart full of love and reverence. Hannah wore a plain blue dress she had sewn herself, her prayer kapp neatly in place as always.

The bishop continued, "Marriage is a blessed union, one that requires devotion, forgiveness, and unwavering faith in Gott and each other."

As was customary, the couple did not exchange personal vows. Instead, Bishop Samuel asked, "Eli, do you promise before Gott and these witnesses to be a loving and faithful husband to Hannah, to support and care for her in sickness and in health, as long as you both shall live?"

"Jah, with Gott's help," Eli responded solemnly.

The bishop turned to Hannah. "And do you, Hannah, promise before Gott and these witnesses to be a loving and faithful wife to Eli, to support and care for him in sickness and in health, as long as you both shall live?"

"Jah, with Gott's help," Hannah answered, her voice clear and sure.

Bishop Samuel nodded approvingly. "By the authority given to me by Gott and this community, I now pronounce you husband and wife."

There was no kiss to seal their union, as was traditional in Englisher weddings. Instead, Eli and Hannah turned to face their community, hands joined at last for a short time, as the congregation broke into a hymn of celebration.

His gaze met hers again, and Eli saw her joy at the promise of a shared life devoted to Gott, family, and community. His own love and happiness reflected back at her, a mirror of . As they walked back down the aisle together, the quiet congratulations of their loved ones surrounded them, demonstrating the strength of their faith and the bonds of their close-knit Amish world.

Eli's heart was filled with pure happiness, and as they walked into the sunlight, he sent a fervent prayer of gratitude heavenward.

As Hannah and Eli made their way out of the hall, hand in hand, her feet barely touched the ground. At least, that's how she felt.

Light and free, utterly effervescent with joy and love. And the love and support of their community surrounded them like a warm embrace, face after face beaming with joy and congratulations.

How different from when Eli first returned home! Now, everyone saw what she had all along. He was gut man, returned to the faith and willing to work to prove his redemption to all.

And now, he had, definitely. Even the most skeptical, including his own father, were convinced. The bishop was one of his most stalwart supporters now, giving his blessing for their spring wedding when others expressed doubt, wanting to see Eli's acclimatization to the community go on longer before he and Hannah married.

But their perseverance, backed by Bishop Zook, won out. And now, it was time to celebrate.

The wedding feast that followed was a joyous affair, filled with laughter, delicious food, and the warmth of family and friends. Hannah sought out Eli's gaze across the crowded tables, again and again. Each shared glance was yet another silent affirmation of their love and commitment.

As the day began to wind down, Hannah and Eli slipped away from the festivities for a moment alone. They stood at the edge of the orchard behind the community hall, the setting sun painting the sky with streaks of brilliant hues. Orange and pink and lavender danced across the sky, the last rays of sunlight turning clouds into gleaming, burnished gold.

"Can you believe it, Mrs. Zook?" Eli murmured, wrapping his arms around her waist from behind. He rested his chin lightly on the top of her head, careful not to disturb her kapp. "We're finally married. Husband and wife."

Hannah leaned back against him, savoring his warmth. She sighed, content and completely at peace.

"It almost feels like a dream," she admitted softly. "A wonderful, beautiful dream. The best I've ever had, actually."

Eli pressed a gentle kiss to her temple. "If it is a dream, I never want to wake up."

As they stood there, watching the sun sink below the horizon, Hannah's mind drifted to the future stretching out before them. There would be challenges, she knew, but with Eli's love and strength, with her own determination and resolve, and above all, with Gott's loving hand guiding them both, she was ready to face anything.

Epilogue

The warm September sun beat down on Eli's back as he guided the plow through the rich earth of a field left fallow the year past. He was breaking the soil now, to better prepare it for next spring's planting. The familiar rhythm of work was soothing, allowing his mind to wander to the incredible changes the past year had brought.

Never, not even in his wildest dreams, did he expect his homecoming to turn into such a bounty of blessings. He paused, wiping the sweat from his brow, and gazed across the field to where Hannah stood, hanging laundry on the line.

Even from this distance, he could see the gentle swell of her belly, evidence of the new life growing within her. Their first child, due to arrive in the new year.

As if sensing his gaze, Hannah looked up, offering him a radiant smile and a wave. Eli's heart swelled with love and gratitude. A year ago, he'd returned to Lancaster County seeking redemption and a place to belong. He'd found so much more - a loving wife, a renewed relationship with his family, and the promise of a bright future.

Eli returned to his work, a contented smile playing on his lips. The harvest ahead would be bountiful, both in the fields and in his life.

As he guided the plow forward, Eli sent up a silent prayer of thanks. For second chances, for love found anew, and for the endless possibilities that Gott offered to them on the road that lay ahead.

With Hannah by his side and their baby on the way, Eli knew their brightest, best days were still yet to come.

The prodigal son not only returned home - he found his true place in the world, rooted in faith, family, and the enduring love of the best woman he'd ever met. His perfect match.

Hours later as the day's work drew to a close, Eli made his way back to the house, drawn by the warmth of home and family. Hannah met him on the porch, a glass of cool lemonade in hand.

He pulled her close and she tilted her head up, smiling at him. As he pressed a gentle kiss to her lips, Eli rested a careful hand to her abdomen, their unborn child between them.

Yes, the best life had to offer was still ahead. Right now, and for the rest of his life, Eli knew he was exactly where he was meant to be. Always and forever.

Hannah hummed softly as she rocked in the sturdy wooden chair on the front porch, cradling little Samuel against her chest. The gentle spring breeze carried the scent of freshly turned earth and blooming flowers, a welcome change from the harsh winter they'd just endured. She gazed out over the distant fields, watching Eli guide the plow through the rich soil, preparing for this year's planting.

A year had passed since their wedding day, and Hannah was still overwhelmed with gratitude for the blessings Gott bestowed upon them. Little Samuel, named after his doting grandfather, arrived in early March in the middle of a winter storm, bringing joy and wonder into their lives.

As if sensing her thoughts, Samuel stirred, his tiny fist grasping at the fabric of her dress. Hannah smiled down at him, marveling at his tiny features, the perfect blend of her and Eli. "Shh, mein kind," she whispered, running a gentle hand over his wispy hair. "Your daed will be finished soon."

Her gaze drifted back to Eli, admiring the strength and purpose in his movements. He'd taken to farming with a passion that sometimes surprised her, given his years away in the English world. But Eli had told her once that working the land made him feel closer to Gott, and she understood that feeling well.

The sound of approaching hoofbeats drew Hannah's attention. Mary Lapp's buggy came into view, and Hannah's smile widened at the sight of her dear friend. Mary, along with both her own and Eli's mamm, was a constant support throughout her pregnancy and these early months of motherhood.

"Gut morning, Hannah!" Mary called as she climbed down from the buggy. "And how is little Samuel today?"

"He's gut, danki," Hannah replied, shifting the baby so Mary could see his face. "Just woke from his morning nap."

Mary cooed over the baby for a moment before settling into the chair beside Hannah. "I brought you some of that tea mixture," she said, producing a small cloth bag. "It helped me so much when I was nursing."

Hannah accepted the gift gratefully. "You're too kind, Mary. I don't know what I'd do without you."

They sat in companionable silence for a moment, watching Eli work in the distance. "You know," Mary said softly, "seeing you now, with your boppli and Eli... it does my heart gut. You've come so far, Hannah."

Hannah felt tears prick at her eyes, remembering the long, dark days after Jacob's passing. "Jah," she whispered. "Gott truly works in mysterious ways. I never thought I could be this happy again."

"Oh!" Mary exclaimed suddenly. "I almost forgot. The women's group is planning a quilting bee next week. We'd love for you to join us, if you're feeling up to it."

Hannah hesitated. "I... I'm not sure," she admitted. "Samuel can be fussy, you know. I don't want to pace up and down the hall the entire time."

Mary patted her arm reassuringly. "Ach, you know there will be plenty of arms to hold him and give you a break," she suggested. "We'd all love to see him, and you'll enjoy the break, I'm sure of it!"

As Hannah considered the offer, she saw Eli unhitch the plow and start walking towards the house. Her heart skipped a beat at the sight of him, dark shirt stretched across broad shoulders, his face lined with honest sweat from his labor.

"Gut morning, Mary," Eli called as he approached. He brushed a quick hand against Hannah's cheek, heedless of their audience, and then gazed lovingly at Samuel. "And how are my two favorite people today?"

Hannah smiled up at him, marveling at how his presence still sent a thrill through her. She hoped it always would.

"We're wunderbaar," she replied softly. "How goes the planting preparation?"

"Gut, gut," Eli nodded. "The north fields are finished and we should be ready to start sowing the western ones in a few days, Gott willing."

As Eli and Mary chatted about the community's planting plans, Hannah looked down at Samuel, now contentedly sleeping once more. She thought about Mary's invitation to the quilting bee, about rejoining the rhythms of community life that she'd stepped back from during the end of her pregnancy and Samuel's early weeks.

"I think," she said, interrupting their conversation, "I'd like to go to the quilting bee next week."

Eli's face lit up with a proud smile. "That's wunderbaar, lieb," he said, squeezing her shoulder gently.

As an animated Mary expounded on the details of the gathering, Hannah relaxed into the soft blanket of peace wrapping around her. This was the life she'd never dared to dream of after losing Jacob.

Finding happiness again with a loving husband, a beautiful child, and a supportive community. Gott blessed her beyond measure, when He brought Eli back to their community and to her side.

And, when He helped her find the courage to let go of the grief and move forward, the way Jacob would have wanted. She rocked her boppli, humming softly as she sent up a silent prayer of thanks, her heart overflowing with utter gratitude at the riches bestowed upon her. Perhaps... if one day they were blessed with a little bruder for Samuel, they might name him Jacob.

And with Eli by her side and Samuel in her arms, Hannah knew that whatever challenges lay ahead, Gott was there beside them, to guide and shelter them, to bring them through the storm and back into the sunlight. Surrounded by love, walking the path in the light of faith, for the rest of their lives.

Thank you so much for reading, I hope you enjoyed the story!

Sign up for my newsletter for new releases, updates, and more.

Please feel free to visit my Facebook page:

https://www.facebook.com/miriambeiler-author

Or email me: **miriam@miriambeiler.com**

Made in the USA
Middletown, DE
28 December 2024